FROM THE FILES OF THE

OTHERWORLDER ENFORCEMENT AGENCY

LYCAN UNLEASHED

TIFFANY ALLEE

Previously released on Entangled's Ever After imprint – January 2013

Entangled Publishing, LLC
2614 South Timberline Road
Suite 109
Fort Collins, CO 80525
Visit our website at www.entangledpublishing.com.

Covet is an imprint of Entangled Publishing, LLC.

Edited by Kerry Vail and Erin Molta
Cover design by Curtis Svehlak
Cover art by DepositPhotos

Manufactured in the United States of America

First Edition January 2013

To Kerry Vail, for pushing me to be the best writer I can be in the kindest way possible.

Chapter One

Bright lights poured over me as I strode up from the parking lot and across the small, dock-style entrance into the boat. I closed my eyes before crossing the threshold and let my attention shift from my five senses to my sixth—as a sensitive, I could feel the powers that otherworlders, or OWs, emitted. "Oh-dub" energy radiated from the boat, but most of it was too far in for me to get a good read. But the shadowy wave of vampire energy was unmistakable—there were several of them inside.

And I could feel the slight pinging of a banshee too, almost too far away for me to sense. Mac would probably be distinguishable from other banshees, especially full-blooded ones. But that wasn't a theory I'd ever had a chance to test, since I'd never been around another banshee.

Casino Merveilleux floated permanently docked on the Fox River. Since it was technically a boat, it could offer gambling games to the residents and visitors of the greater

Chicagoland area. New gambling ships were rare, but with the Chevalier money and influence behind the project, approval had not really been an issue.

Lieutenant Vasquez hadn't mentioned anything specific about the crime scene other than the address, when he'd called me into his office with a brisk, "Astrid, get your ass to this crime scene." So when I found my GPS leading me into the parking lot of a riverboat casino, I was a little ticked. Sure, the lieutenant wasn't exactly the talkative type, but a quick mention of the location wouldn't have been out of order. He'd probably been too pissed about Claude's latest no-notice "vacation" to think to mention it.

Once I got on the ship, the last vestige of marine-style faded, and the feeling of being in a landlocked casino settled over me. Opulence abounded, with rich colors and flashing lights shining through the short hallway leading into the casino proper. Theoretically the Casino Merveilleux could probably still float downriver, but since it had been attached to the dock for a year, at this point it was hard to envision such a change.

The low hum of sound I'd come to expect from such a place was absent. No doubt the police had removed the guests.

I passed a set of elevators and a stairwell. A vampire leaned against a wall with his arms crossed—even if I hadn't been a sensitive, I would have known him for what he was. Fear radiated from vampires, just like sexual appeal draped succubi and incubi. Unlike the insta-lust that succubi and incubi elicited, vampires made people around them instantly want to run the other way. And you didn't have to be a sensitive to feel it.

Some were more bathed in this intimidation aura than others, and this vamp had a decent aura going. He was waiting to bring news to the Magister, no doubt. And to be available to answer questions about the scene for the police. I almost felt bad for the guy. Bringing bad news to one of the most powerful vampires in the country, and the leader of three states full of vamps, wasn't my idea of a fun job.

My sensitive powers were able to discern one vampire from another, although they all smelled somewhat like coffee and appeared draped in shadows that played with my oh-dub vision. Some vamps were more distinguishable than others—and usually that seemed to depend on how powerful they were. This particular vampire was as generic as a vamp could be, and would probably be almost indiscernible from a similarly forgettable vamp.

Others were unforgettable. And that's how I knew that the Magister wasn't on scene. Or at least, he wasn't within my, admittedly short, range.

A uniform moved forward to stop me before I reached the main area of the casino, but I flashed my badge and he waved me through, after writing my name on a form attached to his clipboard. Sweat touched his brow—probably from spending time so close to a vampire with an oppressive fear aura. No police tape blocked my path, but the boat had been emptied—at least the first floor.

It wasn't hard to follow the line of officers and crime scene technicians flowing in and out of the high stakes' poker room. And with one more flash of my badge, I was in.

The smell rolled over me as I approached. Death and the beginning of decay and rot. I swallowed hard and tried not to breathe through my nose. Luckily, the victim had been dead less than a day. Most of the really good smells were just getting started.

With Claude out of town, I'd expected to spend the day doing paperwork. And I would have been okay with that. Not that I'd ever let anyone know, if I could help it. Cops were supposed to love being out in the field, but I was perfectly happy going out only to check over scenes that had already been secured.

The victim had been killed before he was staked to the back wall of the room—feet dangling only a few inches off the ground—that much was obvious. But a stake through the chest—despite the old rumored ways to kill a vampire—probably hadn't killed him. Vampires had to be drained of most of their blood or beheaded to actually die.

His throat had been slit, and that appeared to be the cause of death, but there was very little blood soaking into the carpet beneath him. He'd definitely been dumped here. Pinned against the wall, he had some sort of spikes sticking out of his wrists and chest. His arms were splayed out, but the spike through his chest provided the actual support for the body. Blood covered his neck, soaking his now-dried shirt in starchy red, but very little touched the garish carpet below.

No wonder Vasquez was pissed. The highest ranking vampire on the force, and the unofficial attaché to the vampire community, decides to take the week off a day before someone dies on a casino ship owned by the most powerful vampire family in the tri-state area.

The level of annoyance my partner could draw out of me while not even in the same town was amazing. Most cops didn't have that problem, I was sure of it. Then again, most people weren't partnered with a vampire who considered them to be a long-lost little sister.

Mac and her twitchy new partner, Kurt Jarvis, had beaten me here. By the looks of it, just barely. Jarvis was still removing his winter gloves. Mac was questioning a lab tech within an inch of his life while Jarvis's gaze roved the carpet for evidence.

As a banshee, Mac radiated a certain power that never failed to draw my attention. She didn't sound like a banshee to my oh-dub senses, but something like a wind chime. Sensitives like me felt otherworlder energy often, so unless the OW was actually using his or her powers or was particularly powerful, the OW usually faded into the background of my senses. And many times, I couldn't actually get a read off of an oh-dub unless I was close and concentrating.

Unlike Mac, the tech being questioned seemed human, at least from a distance. As did Mac's new partner, Kurt Jarvis. But Jarvis wasn't human. Not even close.

Mac nodded to me and gave me something close to a small smile when I approached—practically a hug and a kiss from the woman. Jarvis spared me a quick glance before returning his gaze to the floor.

"What do we have?" I asked.

"Dead guy looks like a vamp," Mac said grimly. "Still no ID, but we haven't been able to search the body yet. Techs are still pulling evidence."

I glanced at the body and took a couple of steps away from Mac and Jarvis. Jarvis's jerky motions were distracting, but I reminded myself that he couldn't help it. As an imp, he acted like a man on three pots of coffee. His presence was a bit unsettling if a person was at all nervous or paranoid—and cops were always paranoid—but his speed and cleverness were helpful. Imps were an odd type of otherworlder. They were fast and seemed to uniformly have cunning minds, but they weren't much stronger than a human. And they were as easy to kill as any normal, if you could get them to hold still long enough. But their quick minds and movements made them good cops. And other than the twitchiness, they blended in with normals more easily than most oh-dubs.

Closing my eyes, I tried to ignore the smell that pressed my stomach into my throat, the murmurs of cops and techs around me, and the weight of the eyes watching me.

Mac's power sang, but it was unique, identifiable. Easy to separate. Jarvis also pulsed, in the strangely erratic way imps did. Like a strobe light—a subdued one.

And something else. Yes. Shadowed and dark, hungry but not fierce in the way lycanthropes were—and smothering it all: intimidation and terror.

Vampire.

I concentrated on that thread of Other, and watched the energy that covered the victim. The darkness—like a liquid shadow—didn't just touch the outside of his skin. Coated in a bitter scent I could only compare to burnt coffee, it filled him through and through. My eyes flew open. I dropped my left hand to my side and pushed down the embarrassing knowledge of how I'd probably looked—eyes closed and my arm raised toward the dead man.

"Definitely a vampire," I told them. "Looks like someone was trying to give the Magister a message."

"Seems pretty fucking likely. What a damned mess." Mac glared at the victim as if he'd died to personally ruin her night.

Mac waved toward a man in a suit who had walked up to the line. He approached, obviously trying to keep his expression under control. He halted a good ten feet away from us and put his hand over his mouth, eyes wide with shock.

"Oh, yeah." Mac glanced at the vic. "Let's talk over there."

I followed, out of curiosity more than anything. I was here for my sensitive abilities, but that didn't mean I wasn't curious. Jarvis held back, still glancing around the scene in his restless way.

"Can you walk us through what happened here tonight?" Mac said.

"This is the high roller room. It's closed from five thirty until nine thirty every morning—for cleaning. One of the cleaning staff came in at nine, found the…" His eyes darted to the victim. "The man," he finished.

"We'll need to talk to her." Mac made a note.

He nodded.

"So you didn't get any reports of noise or anything from this room earlier?" I cut in. Mac raised an eyebrow at me, but I ignored her.

"No. Nothing. And we have people around here twenty-four hours a day. I don't see how they could have—" His voice broke and he shook his head.

"Snazzy casino like this, you have to have some good security cameras," Mac said.

He nodded, but his skin paled. "We lost power for a half an hour. The whole ship. We'll give you the footage we have of course—"

Mac cursed under her breath, and I glanced back at the vic.

"That's a lot of work for a half hour," I said. But was it, really? Maybe. Maybe not. Not if he'd been killed elsewhere, which the slit throat with minimal blood seemed to suggest.

"Anything special going on last night? Anything different?" Mac asked.

The man shook his head. "Nothing."

"Do you recognize the deceased?" I asked. Sure, he probably would have said it already if he did, but best to ask just in case.

He shot a quick glance at the body and grimaced. "No. I'm afraid I don't. But we get a lot of people through here."

My attention wandered after that, as I approached the cadaver hanging from the wall. It was easier to think of dead bodies that way. Not as people. Not as victims. But as a simple object. A body. A corpse. Not a man.

Or in this case, not a vampire.

I stopped a couple of feet away, grimacing at the smell even though I was getting used to it. Eyes firmly shut, I forced my flittering thoughts into the back of my mind and tried to keep my focus on the energy in front of me.

I breathed slowly and let myself fall into an almost meditative state—or as close as one could get two feet from a dead vampire with a nervous ME tech shifting on his feet nearby.

The corpse was definitely a vampire, and had not just been killed by one. Sometimes that happened—sensitives could pick up the type of powers that had killed a person in addition to the victim's otherworldly aura. In humans, that's all that would linger. It made identifying the killer easier when it worked that way. But too often, things were muddled. Especially with otherworlder victims.

But nothing about this victim felt like anything but vampire, and the energy was soaked through to his bones. I stood still and let my senses open more fully, but I couldn't sense anything but vampire in the area. Dark energy—unmoving because it lingered on a no-longer-living object—saturated the room.

And on the edge of my senses I could feel the other ohdubs. Mac with her odd swirl of power. Jarvis with his pulsing beat—his power was nearly as twitchy as he was. Some of the vampire's power lingered on him too. He must have been in the room longer than I'd thought, and probably closer to the body than he'd want the evidence techs to know. If I'd gotten here a bit earlier I might have snuck a small touch myself.

In order to get something more specific off the body, I'd have to touch it. And the medical man stood close by to prevent that very thing until he'd gotten the okay from his boss.

I frowned. Something else was here too. Vampiric, but different. Clearer. Through my closed lids I could almost see it. A blot in my vision of black, dark and shadowy like all things vampiric. But somehow thicker and blacker than the vampire above it.

I opened my eyes and blinked at the sudden brightness of the room around me. I took a step closer to the body and searched the floor with my eyes. There. Several feet away something shone under a poker table.

"Mac," I called out, and shuffling sounded from behind me as I crouched by the dark wood table leg.

"You got something?" Mac asked.

"You have a glove?"

Mac reached into a pocket and handed me a purple

nitrile glove. I pulled it on even though I didn't intend to touch anything but the floor, and then pointed to a large coin leaning against the inside of the table leg. It had to have rolled there, to get to such an awkward spot at such an angle. Details were difficult to make out in the casino lighting and at our viewpoint, but it didn't look like any poker chip I'd ever seen. And the circular shape looked wrong somehow, imperfect.

"Are you getting anything off of it?"

"Kind of. But to be able to match it to the owner I'll have to touch it—with my skin. Inanimate objects don't carry the juice to radiate much energy."

Mac waved a tech over to take pictures and collect the coin. "We'll get it processed ASAP."

I stood and frowned. "Someone's coming," I murmured. And unlike the dark, inky blackness that signified vampire, this otherworlder's energy shaded the area around it with a silvery tint. Like an afterimage from looking into a bright light or a scene washed in moonlight. And he smelled of fresh air. Where vampire energy moved slowly—and this vampire vic's moved even less than normal since he was dead—the lycanthrope's aura was wild, strong, fierce.

And this particular one, I recognized.

Lycanthropes were similar to werewolves of legend in that they were a heck of a lot stronger than humans, even in their human forms. And while they could shift, it was a difficult process that some never mastered. And the ones who didn't, simply couldn't shift—at least not without the help of a full moon and a pack. The ones who did—well I'd never seen one shift. Although I'd heard stories from paranormal unit veterans—or freak squad veterans, as normal cops liked to call us behind our backs — about the aftermath of violent crimes committed by shifted lycans or lycanthropes.

Those crimes ended with cops struggling to identify pieces of victims.

Mac pulled a small notebook from the inside of her jacket and started making notes. "So we've got a dead vamp hanging in the high-roller room of the fucking Magister's casino ship. This is going to be a shitstorm."

"But it won't be your shitstorm," A low voice said from behind me.

Damn. He was here, all right.

A shiver crawled up my spine. I mentally winced, but kept my face clear. And I could even see the man in my mind's eye. Dark gray eyes that reflected in the right light marked him as a lycan, but the handsome face was a credit to simply awesome genetics. He wasn't overly tall for a man, but not short either. Still, he seemed to pour into a room, filling it with his presence. And he towered over my four-foot-eleven-inch frame. His light brown hair was only a few shades darker than my sandy blond, but his chiseled features in perfect proportion gave him an edge in the looks department. His power was wild and raging like the beast that dwelt within the lycanthrope.

I turned around, just in time to see a flash of pain when his gaze met mine, gone so quickly I might have imagined it.

Mason.

Chapter Two

Snow—large fluffy flakes of it—fell onto my car as I drove back toward my townhouse in the northern suburbs of Chicago. Not the first snowfall of the winter, but the second. The first had fallen a week before and melted in an odd warm-up, making the still unfinished tiny backyard behind my townhouse into a muddy swampland. A state this snowfall would surely remedy. Luckily, at eleven at night, traffic wasn't an issue.

Mason Sanderson. The man poked holes in my defenses. Originally a paranormal unit veteran, he'd moved off the freak squad into a very unpopular internal affairs position after the squad had been taken over by a normal—Lieutenant Vasquez.

I'd missed the lycan after he left, even though we hadn't worked together on a daily basis like I did now with Claude. Missed his serious eyes, his intense expressions, and his ruggedly handsome features.

I sometimes wondered if I hadn't chased him out of the Chicago Police Department and into the OWEA, but that was pretty darn unlikely. It was probably ambition that pushed him into the Otherworlder Enforcement Agency, just like ambition pushed some human cops into the FBI. The man had only kissed me once. And just because it had been the kind of toe-curling kiss people wrote songs about didn't mean it had affected Mason like it had affected me.

He'd called it a mistake.

We'd been friends, I'd thought. Laughed about the same things, chatted after finishing up with crime scenes and at events we had both attended. A few times we'd actually *talked*. About things bordering on serious. But then, it happened. After following me outside on a beautiful night during a Christmas party held at a fellow freak squad member's house, he'd kissed me. And we hadn't talked since. When he'd been forced to talk to me because of cases, his responses had been short. And humorless.

The change had shocked me. Not made of stone, I'd noticed Mason plenty. But the idea that he'd be attracted to me hadn't really crossed my mind. The intense stares I'd occasionally catch him levying in my direction had been purely my imagination. Or just the way he looked. I thought I had been reading too much into it.

Apparently, I'd been wrong.

I shook my head, trying to eliminate thoughts of the man, and pulled into my garage. I trudged into the house, fed my cat, and put on a fresh set of work clothes. I might as well make myself useful. And lazing about my townhouse with thoughts of Mason Sanderson on my mind was hardly useful.

I drove back downtown and reached the evidence lock-up area adjacent to the main police department offices at three twelve, according to the brightly lit clock on my Accord's dash. A lone SUV was in the parking lot as I pulled in, its brake lights shining. When I got out of my car, I saw Jarvis doing the same.

"Hey." I gave him an awkward wave before dropping my hand to my side.

"Hi," he said, voice jovial and a big grin on his face. I toned my smile down a notch. No need to give the imp the wrong idea. Jarvis was a nice enough fellow, but imps in general creeped me out. Far too excitable.

"What brings you here so early—or late?" Jarvis asked. He carried a small box. The last of the evidence.

"Just thought I'd come by and see if I could get a reading off that coin while we still have it. I'm guessing the OWEA is taking over the investigation since Mason stopped by the crime scene," I said.

He waved me ahead and we walked up to the door. "Mac got into it with him after you left. Guess they want to take over. The Magister asked the OWEA to look into it—his boat and all. But we settled on a joint investigation."

As one of the most powerful vampires in the world, the Magister got what the Magister wanted. "Guess he'd want the best out there," I said, not even attempting to keep the sarcasm from my tone.

Jarvis snorted. He opened the door for me, bracing the box he carried against a hip, and we stepped out of the cold into a building that was less cold, if not exactly warm.

The inside of the warehouse was nearly empty, save for one police officer manning the caged-off entrance into the large storage area where evidence was held. A large man, he looked like he was in his early fifties, and though he'd probably been in great shape once, his muscle had faded to fat.

Not everything would have been sent to the chilly, large building so quickly if the OWEA weren't taking over the investigation. Much of it would have made its way to a smaller area in the actual station. But, with the OWEA assuming responsibility, the evidence was no longer the Chicago PD's problem, so it had been sent here.

The big officer behind the desk waved at me. I'd seen him several times before, but he still took down my badge number and had me sign in.

"Should have some evidence delivered earlier from the casino case," I told him.

"They just brought some stuff in about an hour ago." He reached onto a set of shelves directly behind him and grabbed a couple of boxes. "Not sure what all's come in yet." He nodded to Jarvis. "You need to log that?"

"Yep," the imp replied, eyes shifting from object to object in the room in a most unsettling manner. Imps.

I took the boxes to a large table next to the officer's desk and opened the first one. Officer Donaldson handed Jarvis a form to fill out, and then returned to whatever he'd been doing on his computer before I arrived. Given the current hour, I suspected Solitaire.

I closed my eyes and turned so my back was to the officer. I held my hands, palms down, over the boxes and concentrated on my breath. In and out. Slow and steady. There. The coin I'd found at Casino Merveilleux was inside one of the boxes. I could sense the other evidence too. Not its form, but the energies that lingered on the material. The coin had to be made of an older metal, silver or gold or bronze. Those metals held onto energy better than more modern blends. It took a while to soak in, but once it was there, the energy could remain for years.

Besides, with how saturated this coin was, I was almost certain that its owner had held onto it for a very long time. Carried it on his person for decades, at least. Wherever the vampire had gotten it, he had obviously prized the coin.

I frowned. It didn't feel quite like the vampire victim had. It felt older for one, and the dark vampiric energy that clung to it seemed stronger than it had in the man who'd been staked to the wall of the casino. Nothing else in the box pulled at me quite so strongly, so I opened the lid and pulled out the small evidence baggy containing the coin.

It had already been fingerprinted and samples from the surface had been taken, but I left it in the bag anyway. I itched to take it out, handle it to get a better feel for its owner, but I studied it first. The OWEA would want it kept as untouched as possible in case they decided to run additional tests. Unlike most people, I wasn't afraid of Mason Sanderson. But I didn't want to be accused of mishandling evidence either.

The surface was well-worn, and while I didn't recognize the imagery or lettering on the coin, it looked very old. Bronze maybe. I could make out hints of the original pictures, even with how rubbed down they were. The face on one side supported my very-old theory, as if the chipped edges weren't enough. The man's profile revealed a full beard with some sort of headpiece that tied behind his head. Not a modern crown, but regal all the same. And the lettering was odd too, but had been rubbed away so much I couldn't be sure of the alphabet.

The opposite side portrayed what I could only call an angel. But judging from the age of the coin, the winged person with the low slung wrap around his waist might have been something very different. I kept my hands loose around the coin and closed my eyes. A tighter grip would have been better, but not as evidence-friendly.

Otherworlder energy soaked the thing, and I could see and feel it in my mind. Dark and practically dripping from the object, the energy was purely vampiric. And strong. Something about it was almost hypnotic. But there was something else niggling at the edge of my senses. Not vampiric. I needed to get it out of the bag.

"Can I get you some coffee?" A voice asked from behind me, far too loudly.

My eyes flew open, and I almost turned and snapped at the well-meaning officer. "No, thank you. I'm fine," I said, instead. Couldn't he see that I was working?

"Well, I'll be right back," he said, then disappeared into a door near his desk. I took a deep breath, setting the coin back into the box. I replaced the lid and bit my lip. A vampire owner for sure. I was willing to bet that it wasn't the vampire who had been strung up—the owner had to be older and more powerful than the victim had seemed—so who did it belong to? In reality, even if the spot of blood marring the coin's surface belonged to the victim, that didn't necessarily mean that it was owned by the killer.

But I found that unlikely. The vampire who'd owned the coin had held onto it for decades, if not centuries. To keep something—probably on your person—for that long…no. The owner wouldn't have simply left it on the ground. He would have come back for it. He would have searched for it. Unless he couldn't come back to that room for some reason, like because he'd just hung a body over a poker table.

I shook my head. It didn't matter, not really. The murdered vampire was Mason's problem now. I'd file my report and let him handle the rest. Or let him and Mac arm wrestle for it.

But, just a small touch wouldn't hurt anything. And Mason would likely want information sooner rather than later. With that thought in mind, I reopened the box and pulled the coin out. I turned to wave Jarvis over. But, to my surprise, he already stood right behind me, watching the coin with interest.

"I'm going to touch this to get a better reading. You're going to observe so if needed, you can testify to the fact that I didn't manhandle it or dip it in blood, or whatever."

Jarvis frowned. "Are you sure that's a good idea? Shouldn't you wait until the OWEA confirms they've already done their testing?"

I glared at the coin. I needed to touch it. Just a few seconds and I'd be able to ID the vamp if they could find him. I was sure of it. "It'll just be for a sec."

Jarvis took a step back, as if my decision would somehow contaminate him. I gripped the edge of the baggy, ready to slip it open. Then a pop sounded, and the world went black.

A hard, angry scowl on a very handsome face was the first thing I saw when I opened my eyes. I scowled back, or at least gave it a go.

"Astrid? Can you hear me?" Mason asked, voice rough as if he gargled with gravel. For all I knew, he did. Would be fitting, some sort of tough guy thing.

"If you keep scowling, your face is going to freeze that way," I muttered.

A hint of a smile touched his face, and he let out a long breath. "You scared us there for a minute."

I snorted. Yeah, the day I scared Mason Sanderson was the day I could…well something equally unlikely—like pigs would fly.

"What do you remember?"

I glanced around, taking in my surroundings, the oddness of the situation finally hitting me. I was lying on a hospital bed, in what looked like the ER at county. How had I gotten here? My mind whirred, trying to come up with an explanation, a memory.

"You were in the evidence locker," Mason said, his voice soft, encouraging.

"Yeah. Crap. I remember. I went in to look at the coin. Wanted to see if I could get anything off it before you guys wrestled the case away from Vasquez."

Mason ignored my jibe. "Talk me through it."

"I got there the same time as Jarvis—oh, Jarvis." I hadn't even thought of the imp. Great person I was. "How is he? And the other officer?"

"Everyone is fine," Mason said impatiently. "Keep talking."

The more certain of my health he was, the bossier he seemed to get. I frowned. "Jarvis and I went in. I decided—"

To tell or not to tell Mason that I'd decided to remove the coin from the bag? No. Lying about it would be wrong.

Besides, Jarvis had probably already ratted me out. "I decided to take the coin out of the evidence bag."

"Why?" Mason betrayed none of his feelings in his tone.

"Because I wanted to see if I could get a signature on it, see if I could use it to identify the vampire it belonged to," I said.

"And did you? Get a read on the coin?"

"I didn't get a chance to touch it. I started to pull it from the bag, and that's when I heard a loud noise. A popping sound. But…"

Mason watched me, finally raising his eyebrows and nodding slowly for me to continue.

"I did feel something else on the coin, even through the bag. Not vampiric." I shook my head and puzzled over what I could remember of the sensation. "It was similar to how a witch would feel, but off somehow. Or maybe it just felt off because it was in the bag, I don't know."

"The sound you heard, was it a gunshot?"

"No. Sounded more like a firecracker. Were Jarvis and the other officer knocked unconscious too?"

He leaned back in his chair. "Yes. And the power went out in the building—also in a couple of buildings nearby."

"Disabling the cameras," I said. Crap. Just like the casino.

"Yes. How are you feeling?"

That was a good question. I swallowed and touched a sore spot on my head. "I'm fine," I said. And I was. Not like a headache and a scratchy throat mattered much in the grand scheme of things.

"You want to take a little ride with me?"

Oh hell, did I ever. I met his gaze, searching for a glimmer of amusement, but saw only his intense eyes that never failed to make my stomach clench and my mouth water. "Sure," I managed.

The sun had barely peeked out onto the city when we left the hospital. It felt like days had passed, but I must have been only unconscious for an hour, at the most. I wasn't entirely surprised when we pulled up to the morgue.

"Is this guy even going to be out of the bag yet?"

"Killed on the Magister's property in such a public way? They probably called in Martinson."

I took a long drink from the bottle of water Mason had produced for me on our way out of the hospital. Then I followed Mason into the building.

They had, in fact, called in Dr. Martinson. And he looked every bit as unhappy to be called in at dawn as any nine-to-fiver could look.

"What do we got, Doc?" Mason asked as soon as we reached the room where autopsies were conducted. Dr. Martinson stood next to a table, notebook in hand and autopsy gear still covering his undoubtedly nice slacks and button-up shirt.

The body was covered. Had he already completed the autopsy? In record time, if so.

"Detective—excuse me, Agent Sanderson. Detective Holmes." He nodded to us in turn. The consummate professional. "I just completed the autopsy. No toxicology yet, of course. But I do have COD for you."

"Slit throat?" I asked.

"Yes, Detective. To put it succinctly. Though it wasn't what I'd call a clean slice. We have repeated cuts, and some damage that I can't say for sure came from the knife. But it's difficult to say considering how much they cut into the neck. I'll be taking a closer look at the wounds." Dr. Martinson paused to gather his thoughts, no doubt to offer us a level of detail that would make our eyes glaze, but Mason interrupted.

"Anything unusual about the death? The state of the body?"

I had to give Martinson credit; he didn't even blink at Mason's questions. "Other than the fact that he was staked to the wall with large chucks of wood? Yes, several things. First, he was hung post-mortem, although it wasn't long after his death. He also appears to have been tortured before he was killed."

"Tortured how?" I asked.

The doctor tugged at the cloth covering the victim, revealing his skin down to his waist. The gaping wound in his chest, left from the stake used to hold him in the wall, was the first thing I noticed. Dark circular shapes were the second.

I took an involuntary step forward and my breath caught in my throat. The circular marks—three of them—had been burned in a symmetrical curved line below his collarbone. One, perfectly centered on his sternum, was directly below his neck. The other two also fell below the collarbone to either side. And I recognized the shape.

"The coin," I said.

Mason leaned in to examine the coin marks, and to Dr. Martinson's obvious disgust, sniffed the victim's chest.

"Are you sure this is from the same coin?" Mason asked.

"Or its twin." How many super-old coins exactly like the one we'd found could there be? Two of the burns showed the front of the coin, while the third in the center revealed what I assumed to be an angel on the back. "But these…these are more detailed. Strange. It's like the detail that was rubbed off the coin is showing perfectly here." I could see the lines in the wings, as detailed as the day the coin was minted, if I had to guess.

"Can you sense anything else? Magic? Anything odd like you sensed on the coin?"

I took a deep breath and glared at Mason. It wasn't his fault, but I so hated touching dead people. I placed my hand on the chest, with part of it grazing the coin-shaped wound. Then I closed my eyes.

The oddly cold feeling of the flesh under my fingers faded as I concentrated on my other senses. I did my best to ignore Mason, though his power flashed behind me and constantly filled my nose with a fresh, wild scent. I forced my attention to the vampire.

The taste of coffee filled my mouth right away, and I saw the shadowy energy of the vampire on the body, as dead as the vampire it belonged to. Everything about the man's energy was generic, and I grimaced. Put this man in a crowd of average vamps and I'd never be able to pick him out.

Some otherworlders—powerful ones especially—were distinctive in their energies. My partner Claude's power tasted like coffee, but with a touch of mocha. The Magister tasted like cream with a touch of coffee added. His son, Nicolas, had energy so bitter that after I'd met him I'd stayed off coffee for days.

The victim's energy swirled beneath my fingers, moving very little, like a stagnant pond. That, if nothing else, would have told me he was dead. But a foreign energy intruded. Heat touched my fingertips, and I almost pulled my hands back, but the slight burning sensation wasn't physical, and I knew from experience that it wouldn't hurt me. Nonetheless, I bit my lip and concentrated on keeping my hands in place.

"What is it?" Mason murmured, far too close to me. I jumped, just a little, but it was enough to break my skin on skin connection to the vampire.

"Do you mind?"

"Sorry." He held it hands up. I shot him a glare and then turned back to the vamp.

With my eyes open, I traced the cold skin. Then, grimacing in disgust, I touched one of the coin-shaped wounds. Fire crawled up my fingertips, and I yanked my hand back, my body's instinct more powerful than my desire to continue touching the body.

"The coin is enchanted. Spelled. Powerful, too."

Mason was silent for a few seconds, and I took the opportunity to go to the sink to wash my hands. I'd need a shower too. The morgue always made me feel coated in death.

"I thought that was a myth," he said as I dried my hands.

"It's so rare it might as well be." And that was the understatement of the year. Objects could be infused with spells, but said spells nearly always destroyed the object upon completion. And they were difficult as hell to work. But something about this one was different. It wasn't destroying the coin, for one.

"Are you sure? Did you get that off the coin, too?"

"No, which isn't surprising. If a spell isn't active it can be very difficult to detect." I glanced at the body. Something was off about this. Enchanted objects tended to feel a bit like the witch who'd cast the spell, and a bit like the spell itself. The burning might be related to the spell, but I should have felt something relating to the witch. Maybe. Unless the spell was as old as the coin appeared to be, which might explain why the image burned into the body was so clear. It would mirror the coin when it had originally been spelled. But who the heck could work magic like that? The idea of it made my head hurt.

"Did you get anything about the witch who cast it?" Mason asked.

"No." I almost said more, but stopped myself. I didn't really know anything. And my guesses wouldn't help. Mason had witches on his payroll who'd do a better job of it.

I was no witch.

I stared in disgust at the moldy bowl of something that might have once been cereal in the officer's hand. "No. I told you I can't sense anything off that stuff. I'm not taking it out of the bag and touching it."

Kowalski grimaced and carried himself, and his zip-locked bag of crap, away with him. It was amazing, with how long otherworlders had been fully integrated into the police force in Chicago—one of the first cities to allow all oh-dubs to work at all levels—that some officers still didn't understand how otherworlder powers worked. Half the humans—and even a few of the more ignorant nonhumans—assumed my powers were far more encompassing than they actually were. I wasn't clairvoyant for crying out loud. And I couldn't get images off objects like a psychometrist could. I could feel energy. That was it.

Which was damn useful in most situations, if not in a

fight.

That usually led to me being corralled in the station until I was needed, and then I was only allowed out with Claude. No matter how proficient I became with my sidearm, I was viewed as weak by my fellow oh-dubs. Practically human. But that was A-Okay with me. I liked what I did—identifying oh-dub energy on victims and objects. I was good at it. Just because I didn't have the desire to chase after murderers and stare victim's families' in the eye, didn't mean I wasn't a good cop.

I finished writing the report on the riverboat casino crime scene, and the additional impressions I'd noted when touching the coin through plastic in the evidence locker. Evidence, whether physical, psychic, or sensed, had to be catalogued with the same amount of detail.

I spared a quick glance at Vasquez's office. Mason and a couple of other OWEA agents had gone in with Vasquez nearly an hour before. I'd kept my attention away from the door as much as possible, but I couldn't help the occasional glimpse at the men inside. For one, even though the case was no longer my problem, I was still curious about it. For another, despite my best efforts, I couldn't ignore Mason Sanderson if my life depended on it.

The door clicked open and I tore my eyes away to stare at the police report I'd polished within an inch of its life, praying that Mason hadn't seen my interest. My heart thumped faster in my chest as footsteps approached me from behind. But it wasn't Mason who spoke.

"Holmes," Vasquez said, "we need to talk."

I followed Lieutenant Vasquez back to his office, snagging a copy of my finished report off of the printer on the way. Mason waited inside, but the other two agents were gone. They'd probably left while I was pretending I wasn't interested in what was happening in the office behind me.

Vasquez gestured for me to sit, a hard expression on his face. Mason remained behind me by the door, his arms crossed and his expression closed off.

"What's up?" I asked, heart racing now for a different reason. Tension saturated the air, and I had the sudden feeling that it was directed at me.

"How are you feeling? Any side effects from whatever spell knocked you down?" Vasquez asked.

"I'm fine. Just a bump on the head."

"Good." He crossed his arms, his gaze never dropped from mine. "Did you remove evidence from the lock-up?"

My mouth dropped open. "Excuse me?" That my voice stayed at its normal, polite level was a testament to my mother and the years of training she'd insisted on, because I couldn't remember the last time I'd been so angry.

Then again, I'd never been accused of misconduct before.

"The coin disappeared from the lock-up," Mason said. "According to our Covenant contact, it's likely that the spell was activated from inside the building. The spell knocked out the power and cameras in the building too, so it couldn't be tracked. Someone sets off the spell, an accomplice comes in while everyone is knocked out to grab the coin." Mason's voice lacked emotion, but his words hit me like a brick.

"So you think that I…" I couldn't get the words out. Betrayal flooded me. After all this time, Vasquez could really suspect me of this? And Mason. God, the idea of him thinking I would remove evidence like that made my eyes suddenly burn. I swallowed hard.

"No," Vasquez said firmly. "We don't. But this does make the lot of us look like prize idiots—best case scenario. I'm sorry, Astrid, but I'm going to have to ask you to take a few days off until the inquiry is complete."

I took a deep breath. "You don't think I did anything wrong, but you're going to make me take leave anyway? You know how that'll look, don't you? Everyone will think—"

"They won't," Mason cut in, deep tones reassuring despite the situation. "It's not just you."

Vasquez shot Mason a glare for butting in to what he no doubt viewed as his conversation. "Exactly. Jarvis is going to be on administrative leave, too. As is the officer who was on duty at the evidence locker. It's just for a couple of days."

I clenched my hands together in my lap to prevent myself from fidgeting. "That spell might have been set off by someone in the building, but that doesn't mean it couldn't have been attached to an object, and was set off when one of us inadvertently touched it. It could have even been set to a timer—sort of. A very iffy kind of timer." I grimaced under their scrutiny. "Magical timers aren't exactly accurate."

"Be that as it may, we have to look into it." And Vasquez's words were final, his tone brooked no argument.

My career was on the line. Vasquez didn't say it, but I knew that it was true. And their inquiry was likely to turn up my family history, which would put me smack dab on the top of their suspect list. Heck, even if my career wasn't officially damaged, with my family ties, Vasquez wasn't going to trust me as much. Not with how perfectly those ties could have helped me remove that evidence.

Not that I was the only one at risk here. Guilt twinged in my chest when I thought of Donaldson and Jarvis. They didn't deserve this any more than I did.

"Fine," I said icily, forcing the veneer of politeness and formality my family had drilled into me around myself. And for once, I was happy to have the defense. "I'll be at home."

"I'm going to need your badge and sidearm," Vasquez said.

I wanted to bristle and fight, but that would only make me look worse. Shoulders stiff, I pulled my gun from its holster and placed it on the desk, then tossed my badge next to it. Ignoring the two sets of eyes that followed my movements, I turned and left.

My silent house greeted me when I got home, but I was quickly inspected by my cat—who I suspected was more interested in the odd hour of my return than in me.

I stayed in my quiet townhouse as the darkness settled in over the trees in my backyard. And I stayed home through the nightly news. The vampire's death was a top story, though the details were kept hazy. A body, found on the casino ship owned by the vampire's Magister. Foul play suspected. The victim's species wasn't specified.

When the ten o'clock news ended, the restless feeling that had crawled over me since I had left the station inundated my every cell. I had to do something. Anything. And I had to get out of my townhouse. Despite Vasquez's reassurance that I wasn't in any trouble, if whoever took the coin wasn't found, the police department would need a scapegoat.

My career was on the line—or at the very least my reputation. And I knew where I had to go.

I grabbed my personal firearm—a 9mm I'd owned since before I joined the force. I didn't think I'd need it, but I felt naked without a gun nearby since I had carried one for several years.

When I got in my car, I shoved the unloaded gun into my glove compartment along with a box of bullets. Then I locked the glove box. I felt better with the gun there even though I didn't intend to take it out or load it. It had been a long time since I'd travelled without a sidearm, but a gun in my car would have to be good enough.

Mason wasn't going to help me easily. I had to give him a reason to let me in, something only I could help him with. He didn't have any motivation to let me in on the investigation as things stood now, and had every reason not to. Sure, he'd kissed me once. But he'd never followed up on it, had called it a *mistake*. That one moment of closeness would hardly convince him to let me back into the investigation. In fact, bringing up that incident would more than likely end with me kicked out of his house, if not arrested for whatever charges he could come up with to keep me out of his hair for a couple of days.

No. The personal angle wasn't going to help me. I had to come up with something else—something that would convince him beyond a doubt that he had to let me in. Even better, that he had to have me working alongside him. My mind rebelled at putting myself into a situation that would almost certainly put me more out in the field than I was used to, or comfortable with, but I couldn't stand idly by while my career came to a screeching halt.

I parked on the street in front of Mason Sanderson's sprawling house. Steeling my spine, I walked up his driveway.

Light from small lamps lining the drive reflected off the concrete, creating odd shadows as I trudged to the flagstone walkway leading to the front door.

Mind racing, I made my way up the steps and lifted the knocker and let it drop back onto the door twice.

Should I ring the doorbell, or would that be too obtrusive? I crossed my arms, blew a large sigh into the chilled air, and watched it puff around me. Surely he wasn't sleeping already?

My heart dropped into my stomach. What if he had someone else here? What if he didn't live alone anymore? Hell, he'd worked for the OWEA for a couple of months, and IA for a year before that. A lot of news made its way through the police grapevine, but not everything. Mason Sanderson could be married now, for all I knew.

Just as my mind was making the leap from wife to possible children, the door opened. Framed in the doorway, Mason stood stiffly. His expression was still hard, but somehow less distant than it had been at the station.

For a beat, I just stared at him, unable to yank my gaze from his. The gray eyes I'd seen soften only once, in passion. They'd reflected under the moon the night he kissed me. The mouth that now formed a hard line had softened so perfectly against my lips. Brushing against his forehead, his hair was still damp from his shower. And the way the black T-shirt stretched across his muscular chest made my mouth dry.

"What are you doing here, Astrid?" he asked, breaking me from my spell.

I cleared my throat and stared at the hardwood beneath his sock-covered feet. "I need to talk to you."

"I don't think that's a good—"

"Please," I said, glancing at his eyes quickly before returning my gaze to the floor.

"All right," he said gruffly. "Come in."

I scanned Mason's hallway. I'd never actually been here before, and I prayed that he didn't ask me how I knew where he lived. I'd looked him up once. Not long after the kiss.

Dumb.

The place was impressive, nearly as nice as the house my parents lived in. The house I had been banished from at far too young an age. I pushed back a rush of anger at that memory, and concentrated on my surroundings. Mason's home was warmer than my parents'. Browns and other natural shades covered the surfaces of his furniture and walls, and the decor was simple. It was too nice for a cop's house, especially in a nice suburb so close to the city.

Were our backgrounds as dissimilar as I'd always thought? Mason had never struck me as well off. Something about his gruff exterior, plain clothes, and two-day old shave always made me think blue collar. Not in a bad way, but in a rough, manly sort of way.

Get a grip, Astrid.

We reached the living room and Mason stopped and turned to me. "I can't get you back to work, if that's why you're here. Vasquez doesn't listen to me if he doesn't have to. And I have no jurisdiction over what the Chicago PD does anymore."

"Do you think I took the coin?" I asked, hating the way the break in my voice gave my emotions away.

"No."

Relief flooded through me at his hesitation-free answer. A small piece of me had wondered if he thought so little of me, but his simple response pushed my battered confidence up a bit. "Thank you."

He shrugged and watched me.

I struggled to meet his gaze. "I want you to bring me in. Let me investigate with you."

"Not a chance."

I had the inexplicable urge to ask him why, even though I already knew the answer. "I can help you."

His eyes narrowed. "How? The OWEA has sensitives I can call in if I need to. It would have been...easier to use you. But I can get someone else."

"Maybe. But have any of them handled the coin?"

He gestured for me to continue and then crossed his arms.

"I held the coin. I should be able to identify the owner," I said, the lie pressing against my throat, trying to choke me.

"You managed to get a strong enough reading off that coin to be able to do that without physically touching it?" he asked, eyebrow raised. "I thought you said you hadn't touched it with your bare skin when we talked at the hospital."

Mason wasn't an idiot. He knew how rare that would be for a sensitive, even one as strong as me. "I told you, the owner held that coin—probably almost constantly on their person—for decades, maybe centuries," I evaded. Not a lie. Not exactly a lie, anyway. I suppressed a cringe. When Mason found out about the omission—and there was no doubt in my mind that he would eventually—I didn't think he would care that the lie was omission-only.

"It's not a good idea."

"I need to clear my name." I swallowed hard and put

strength into my voice. "It's my reputation on the line. Maybe my badge. I should have that right."

Mason took a deep breath and stared at me. I struggled not to squirm under his steady gaze. Finally he nodded. A short quick motion that seemed more to himself than to me. "You'll do what I say, when I say it. And you will have to work as a consultant. It's highly irregular, but I do need a sensitive for this case. I can make it fly if I have to. But you'll follow my orders to a T. And you won't breathe a word of it to anyone."

Elation rushed through me, tempering my annoyance at his tone. He wasn't asking me to bow to his demands; he was stating them as if my choice in the matter was nonexistent.

"Deal." I held my hand out and Mason stared—as if it might turn into a snake—for a few seconds. I almost withdrew, but finally he took my hand with his own. His lycan energy rushed around me, made all the more clear and distracting because of our physical contact. I dropped his hand, and an expression flashed across his face too quickly for me to identify. But any expression on the man was a rarity.

It suddenly struck me that I might not be the only one who still thought about that kiss.

Chapter Three

Overcast skies still hung low over the city when Mason came to pick me up Sunday morning, and snow barriers surrounded the slushy roads. The air was cold when I stepped out of my house after his curt knock, but not biting like it would be when the clouds cleared. I clutched my to-go coffee mug against my coat and locked the deadbolt.

"We got an ID," he said without preamble as we walked down the sidewalk.

"Good." I reached for the door handle but Mason beat me to it. He opened my door and gestured for me to get in. I blinked at him dumbly for a few seconds, then hopped in the SUV. He shut the door soundly behind me.

He wasn't hitting on me. I was certain of that. Was he just being polite? I knew that Mason was a bit old school with certain things, but I couldn't remember the last time I'd had a man open a building door for me, let alone a car door.

"The name's Jake Stone. His wife ID'd the body last

night. She's expecting us this morning."

I nodded and decided this wasn't the best time to ask about his chivalry. I could feel him next to me, and his power was a little distracting. I'd get used to it—hopefully sooner rather than later. The first week I'd worked alongside Claude, I'd been hopelessly distracted by his power signature humming along beside me. But I'd gotten used to him, so his aura had faded into the background, leaving me free to pay attention to the rest of the world. But Mason's was still fairly fresh and new, and very different from the vampire's. Wild and glinting, not dark and controlled. And the fresh, outdoorsy scent of his energy comingled with his scent as a man in a very delicious way.

"What?" I asked, feeling stupid. Distracted again.

"I said, make sure to let me do the talking. I don't want word getting back to Vasquez about the little sensitive coming to question witnesses with me."

The "little" comment made me want to respond with a biting retort, but I calmly replied, "Okay," instead. *Polite over spite*, my mother's voice intoned in my head.

I took a sip from my to-go mug. The coffee—thick with cream and sugar—slid smoothly down my throat. Familiar, soothing, and a wonderful distraction from Mason's energy.

The vampire's wife lived in the city. Up and coming was how a real estate agent would describe the neighborhood. Nice, but with decay and age lingering along the edges and coating a few of the buildings not yet renovated. I chewed on the inside of my lip and tried to get my mind around a middle-class vampire.

"What is it?" Mason asked, taking in my expression after parking on the street.

"Nothing. It's just—" I waved my hand around. "I don't think I've ever met a vampire who wasn't rich."

Mason snorted. "Well, many of them have been around long enough to accumulate a lot of wealth. Maybe this one's younger."

"Maybe." That would also fit his very ordinary power signature. While most never got truly powerful like Claude or the Magister, the older ones tended to feel more unique. I suspected age played no small part in that truth.

We crossed the slushy street and Mason lingered near me. No doubt at the ready in case I slipped in the slush and fell on my butt. The man was far too chivalrous to live in the modern day. A sexy, broad shouldered antique.

The house we approached was one of the nicer on the street. Although it was difficult to see the differences with everything covered in snow, the paint job was a bit newer. And all of the original windows had been replaced with energy efficient ones.

I paused at the door, and Mason reached around me to knock. His arm brushed mine, and even though we were both covered—me in my thick winter coat and him in a much lighter jacket—I could feel his power caress me. My heart raced, and it annoyed me that he could probably hear it.

"You should let me feel places out before you do that," I muttered.

"What?"

"Claude always has me check out buildings with my powers before knocking or entering."

"Well, I'm not Claude," he said, and there was an edge to his voice.

I glared at him from under my eyelashes, but before I could come up with an appropriate response, the door opened.

The woman's beauty and pure sexual force would have told me what she was, even if my sensitive powers weren't on high alert. Her energy tasted like strawberries and my fingers tingled—both sure signs of a succubus. Hair as dark as coal draped her face and hung all the way to her waist. Hazel eyes, rimmed in red and swollen from crying, peered out at us. She licked her full lips before she spoke. "Yes?"

"I'm Agent Sanderson, and this is Astrid Holmes. She's helping out on your husband's case," Mason said. "We spoke on the phone last night?" His voice had lowered to its least menacing growl, but the man still sounded like a predator.

She flinched almost imperceptibly and stepped back. "Of course. I'm Mary Stone. Please come in."

We walked through her Pottery Barn-decorated home and sat at her dining room table. I had to hop in a most unsophisticated fashion to get onto the tall chairs surrounding the large table, and annoyance flashed through me as the tall succubus sat gracefully. Then Mason started in with the questions.

"I know that this is a rough time, Mrs. Stone, but if you could run us through the last day you saw your husband, it would be helpful."

Mary nodded and dabbed at her eyes with a tissue. The succubus managed to be beautiful even after crying. "It was just a normal day. Jake got up and went to work and so did I. He said he had to go out at around seven and he left."

"He didn't tell you where he was going?" Mason pulled out a notebook from the inside of his jacket and made a quick note.

"No. I assumed it was for work." Eyes wide like a frightened baby animal, she looked every bit the innocent. I wasn't sure I bought it, and a slight narrowing in Mason's eyes made me think he didn't either.

"Your husband worked in a law office, as a paralegal?" Mason asked.

"Yes."

"Did he have to work nights often?"

She took a sip of water from her glass, hands trembling. "No. He didn't usually work nights."

"Did he go out in the evenings like that a lot? Without telling you where he was going?" Mason pressed.

"No, but I—"

"Then why didn't you ask him where he was going?" Mason said, the aggression in his leaning stance growing more pronounced.

The succubus was the same height as Mason, within an inch or two, but as he shot out questions that she struggled to answer, she seemed to shrink, and he appeared to glower over her. Their energy pulsed around me, and I got lost in it for a few moments, missing some of his questions. Tears built behind the woman's eyes, but Mason didn't seem to notice.

"I'm just having a hard time understanding why you'd let him walk out that door without knowing where he was going, Mrs. Stone," Mason said. His voice was still low, but I could feel the danger lurking there. Controlled violence. And Mary Stone could obviously feel it too. Her face crumpled and she drew back into herself like she expected Mason to strike her.

I stood, hopping off the pub-sized chair in as dignified

a manner as I could manage. "Thank you, Mrs. Stone. We appreciate your time. We understand that you're grieving right now and probably have funeral arrangements to make, so we'll come back another time." I held out my hand to the succubus and she shook it, her clammy hand flimsy and weak against my firm grip.

"Thank you," she gasped, trying to control her tears, which were fast dissolving into outright sobs.

Mason gaped at me for a second before he snapped his mouth and notebook shut. "Thank you, Mrs. Stone," he muttered, and then he followed me to the door.

"What the hell was that?" Mason asked after we were back in his car.

I shrugged, still in shock that he'd opened my door for me yet again, even though he practically radiated anger. Courtesy must have been driven into him as much as acting politely had been driven into me. "She wasn't going to give us anything."

"I had her ready to crack."

I eyed him levelly. "No. You had her scared and stressed, and even less likely to tell you anything. The woman just lost her husband. Don't you know how to question people without scaring them witless?"

He shoved his key into the ignition and the SUV roared to life. "Intimidation is a proven questioning technique."

"Yes. And one you're undoubtedly good at," I said dryly. "But it's not the only technique and not the best one for questioning a woman who just lost her husband. A woman who isn't even a suspect."

His brows drew together and he pulled out onto the street. "Close family—spouses in particular—are always suspects."

"Yes. But it isn't exactly likely that she nailed him to that wall. Last I heard, succubi don't have super strength."

"That doesn't mean she didn't do it with help."

I crossed my arms and glared at him. "I'm not saying that she doesn't know more than she's letting on. And she might well be involved. But coming at her with a bit of compassion and kindness would have gotten us more information."

"If you hadn't butted in—something I specifically told you not to do—we might have more information right now," he said, but doubt touched his voice.

I didn't press the issue. He'd just dig his heels in deeper. Stubborn ass. Instead, I asked, "Where to now?"

"We'll question some of his coworkers." He gave me a sidelong glance, full of meaning. "And by we, I mean me."

It took every bit of my considerable self-control not to roll my eyes at him. *Think like a sailor if you must, my dear, but you will speak like a lady if you want to be treated like one.* My mother might have been right, but Mason sure tempted my control.

Jake Stone's direct supervisor and the two co-workers we spoke to didn't know of any projects that would have required Jake to leave his house that evening. The firm was vampire-owned—by the Magister's own company—and run by his son Nicolas. And I got the distinct feeling that even though Jake was a paralegal and not an attorney, his vampire status gave him a lot more leeway in his position than he would have gotten if he were a human. Even in the world of vampire companies, sometimes it came down to who you knew, not what you knew.

We headed to lunch after leaving Jake's law office. It was almost one thirty by the time we arrived at The Grill House, so the crowds were thinning and we were seated quickly.

Mason eyed me over his menu from across the booth. "So, what do you think?"

"I don't know yet."

He raised his eyebrows. "No theories?"

"Sure. But I'm trying to keep an open mind." *Never assume.* I didn't always stick to the first thing Claude had taught me when I was assigned as his partner, but I tried.

Mason folded his menu and placed it on the table, flush with the corner. "I think we're probably dealing with some sort of vampire turf war."

"Perhaps." I focused on my menu. It was difficult to pay attention to Mason and the food choices at the same time as we were in such close proximity to several other oh-dub patrons. A salamander was nearby—I could feel the signature heat. And if I wasn't mistaken, a selkie was close too. The scent of saltwater came through subtly, mostly overpowered by the smell of fresh air carried by Mason.

"Well, we have a dead vamp who belonged to the local Magister. He was displayed at the Magister's place of business." He leaned forward and caught my eye. "And he was killed in a manner that matches the M.O. of other vampire murders across the country."

I dropped the menu on the table. "When did you make that connection?"

He frowned. "Even before I got to the scene. I mentioned it to Mac. You were there."

"I was distracted." God, he probably thought I was incompetent.

"You're distracted a lot."

I opened my mouth to tell him where he could stick his attitude and then snapped it shut. I didn't have to explain myself to him, didn't owe him an explanation for the bits of conversation I missed. My issues with paying attention were my own.

The waiter saved us from an awkward silence. The bright-eyed young man asked for our orders with a big smile on his face.

"Steak," Mason said. "Salad, and baked potato," he added. "Coke to drink."

"How do you want it cooked?"

"Rare," he said, and his gaze flashed back to me.

Shivers ran down my spine at that look. He could have been talking about sex instead of food for how my body reacted to his gaze.

"And you?" the waiter asked me.

"I'll take a Coke too. And a burger and fries."

"We'll have that out for you soon." The perky young man dashed off to his next table.

"You said there were other victims?" I said, bringing the conversation back to the case before Mason could derail me. "What are the similarities?"

"Vampires with their throats cut for one. And they were all killed by another vampire—or more than one—as far as we can tell. And no bite marks on the bodies. Whoever is killing these vamps isn't feeding off of them."

My stomach dropped. For any other species, killing by cutting a person's throat wouldn't necessarily be enough to tie murders together. But if a vampire killed them all, the likeliness of the same killer increased exponentially. Vampires craved blood like addicts craved drugs. And the scent could be overwhelming for them—particularly the smell of their own kind's blood.

It was why there were almost no vampire doctors or nurses. Not because it was illegal—that would be discriminatory—but because the vampires themselves would not allow their members to be put into such precarious positions. The control it would take for a vampire to resist a small bite with someone pouring their lifeblood out right in front of them…it was difficult to imagine.

Especially if the vampire had cut the throat of the person bleeding to death in front of them—morals wouldn't be a factor.

Mason simply watched as I considered the implications, and I wondered if he could read my thoughts on my face. Claude swore it was an easy thing to do, so I'd worked at schooling my expression. But so often, I simply forgot. Sensory overload did that to a person.

The waiter dropped off our drinks and promised our meals would be out soon.

"Other connections," I asked after he'd moved away again.

"They all seem to have some political motivations. A vampire trying to take over a Magister's position. Repayment for a perceived slight. Things of that nature."

"But not all connected to the same vampire Magister?"

"Nope. We think that the perp is something of a gun for hire. A free agent." He stabbed at the ice in his glass with his straw, loosening it from a large glob of frozen water to something easier to drink around.

"A vampire assassin," I muttered. "Why doesn't the killer take the blood?"

"We think it's to show how tough he is. How powerful."

"He?"

"We have a suspect. But we don't have enough evidence on any of the cases to make an arrest. He goes by Isaiah—no known last name." Mason pulled the straw from his glass and then took a long drink from his Coke. "He's good."

"So someone is either trying to move in on the Magister's territory, or they're sending him a strong message."

Mason stretched, his hands moving behind his head, giving me a great visual of the well-formed muscles that pushed at the shirt binding them. "That's the working theory."

Suddenly warm, I picked up a small dessert menu that was propped up on our table and fanned myself. "It's a good theory."

"But?"

"But it doesn't explain why the wife was so nervous. Why she'd be hiding something from us."

Mason nodded. "Like I said, it's a theory. And she could have been nervous for any number of reasons."

I snorted. "Like an intimidating lycan staring her down?"

A laugh escaped him, short, but it lit up his whole face for a brief moment. "Could be."

"Maybe she thought you were going to change right then and there and eat her." I grinned at the thought. Sensitives weren't the only misunderstood oh-dubs out there, and lycans were especially misunderstood. Something about the ability to change into a beast-man creature that could dismember a limb with one good bite tended to intimidate people. Not that the succubus could necessarily tell what Mason was, like I could, but the man felt like a predator. You didn't need a sensitive's abilities to feel that.

His light expression faltered. "Not much chance of that."

I almost pressed him to explain what he meant, but his expression hardened as I watched. Whatever it was, it wasn't something he wanted to talk about. So I changed the topic to something I knew was safe, and of great interest to Mason.

"So, how about the Bears this year?" Mason was intense about his work, and the first time I'd gotten a peek at the man beneath, it had been during a football discussion.

Mason looked at me quizzically for a second before he relaxed. We chatted about football until the waiter dropped our food off and I let myself sink away from the world while we ate in companionable silence. Allowing my focus to drift, instead of forcing my senses to filter out the excess energies I could see and feel as a sensitive, relaxed me and I could feel the headache that was threatening to ruin my afternoon fade away.

"Are you done?" Mason asked, his voice startling me.

"Oh, yes." I pushed my half-full plate forward and touched my napkin to the corners of my mouth.

Mason frowned at my plate. "No wonder you're such a little thing," he muttered. Then more loudly to me, he said, "You should eat more."

"I'm fine," I insisted.

He glanced at his watch. "We have to leave now, anyway."

"Where to next?" I scooted out of the booth, pausing when he spoke.

"To interview the Magister. Maybe he'll know who has a beef with him."

Chapter Four

I expected Mason to head to the Magister's estate. But instead he drove north out of the city, then west. When he parked in front of Casino Merveilleux, I wasn't entirely surprised, but I was annoyed. Not so much at the location, but at the slithering pulse of vampire power I could feel from within. Even from the parking lot, Luc Chevalier made an impression.

We walked in and took the elevator up to the top floor. The elevator opened into a short but stately hallway that led to a single set of double doors. The vampire guarding the entrance radiated a fear aura at a level I hadn't felt from a vamp in a long time, and every muscle in my body encouraged me to run back into the elevator. I pushed down the urge. This vamp was nothing more than a lackey, a bodyguard for the Magister—as if Luc Chevalier really needed anyone to guard his body. The threat the guard radiated had nothing to do with his actual power. That, from what I could sense, was in a mediocre range.

I glanced at Mason. His jaw was tense, but other than that he didn't react to the vampire. If I were a betting woman, I would put my money on the lycan against a mid-level vamp any day.

Mason flashed his badge at the guard, who examined the identification closely before he nodded and opened the door. He stepped back to allow us entry, and his power licked at me as we passed.

I'd felt the Magister even before we entered the building, but when the door closed behind us, the otherworlder energy in the room washed over me like a flash flood: harsh and powerful and *fast*.

I stopped in my tracks and closed my eyes, breathing slowly to give myself a chance to adjust. I was used to vampiric energy. Claude was nearly as strong as the Magister himself, and I spent most of my waking hours with him. But there were so many powerful vamps in this room that it was a bit of a rush, especially with Mason's contrasting silver-tinged lycan energy swirling. Burnt coffee filled my lungs, overpowering Mason's fresher, more pleasant scent. And waves of shadows rolled through the room, distracting and a bit vertigo-inducing.

And I couldn't escape the sudden harsh realization that this situation was exactly why I hated going into the field.

"Are you all right?" Mason murmured, his mouth only inches from my ear.

My eyes fluttered open and I nodded, shaky from the energy and his proximity. His scent washed over me, a touch of sweat and wildness, soap and cola.

Mason turned his attention to the rest of the room. The

Magister, Luc Chevalier, lounged in a large leather chair behind a desk, hands clasped behind his head. Sitting on the corner of the desk was another vampire I recognized. Nicolas Chevalier, Luc's natural born son from before Luc was turned. A rare treasure among vampires. And according to Claude, a big pain in the ass.

A woman stood to the other side of the desk. But unlike Nicolas, she was behind it, leaning against the wall behind Luc. Her arms were crossed. Although her frame was slight, she looked around five and a half feet tall. Asian, with soft dark hair brushing her shoulders, she would have struck me as quite lovely if not for the threatening aura that seemed to pour from her, beating at us like waves against rocks.

It was difficult to tell the vampires' auras apart with them all together, especially with the punch the Magister carried. But from what I could feel, the tiny woman carried enough power to put even Nicolas to shame. And the Magister's son was no slouch.

Mason introduced himself and shook everyone's hands. I was grateful for his presence. I felt safer, for one. And his lycan energy helped to break up the barrage I was receiving from the vampires. Gave me something different to concentrate on, to cling to. Even though it did little to keep my focus on the interview.

"Astrid," the Magister said, reaching out to take my hand in both of his. His energy flooded over me, almost painful in its strength, and the room and its occupants faded as I fought for focus. He held my hand like we were close friends for an awkward moment, until Mason took a step closer to me.

"So nice to see you, my dear," Luc continued. He

released my hand and stepped back. I nodded politely.

I'd met the vampire Magister a few times during the couple of years I'd worked with Claude, and he had always been polite. But he'd never acted so warmly before. Had he already heard about what had happened? Did he know my badge was in jeopardy?

"Detective, Agent, this is my son Nicolas. And," he added, almost as an afterthought, "his assistant, Min."

Mason shook hands with the other vampires, but I held back, nodding to them in turn. Filtering through their energy was overwhelming enough without physical contact.

"Tell us what you know about the victim, Magister," Mason said.

I shot him a warning glance for his tone, but the Magister didn't seem to notice. Or, more likely, wasn't bothered enough by it to make a scene.

"I met Jake only a few times. He was a decent enough young man, if not particularly powerful or ambitious."

I frowned. "Jake wasn't from here?"

"No. He was a transplant."

Catching where I was going with the question, Mason continued as if I hadn't interrupted. "Isn't that unusual for a younger vampire, to leave his family?"

"Yes, it is. But Jake's wife wasn't particularly popular with his family. He elected to leave Denver around a year ago to join us here."

I gave Mason a small nod when I noticed him glance at me. That made sense. While vampires married outside of the fold occasionally, it was rare. Vampires were long-lived, which gave them time to accumulate large numbers of their kind. But in general, marrying a shorter-lived creature wasn't encouraged, although it was hardly a crime.

I lost myself within my own thoughts and in the pulse of the energy around me. I rubbed my nose, but the smell of burnt coffee wouldn't fade until we left the vampires. When the conversation caught my focus again, Mason had moved on to question Nicolas.

The Magister's son answered Mason's questions with one-word answers where he could, and brief responses otherwise. He'd worked at the same branch as Jake Stone, and was acquainted with the vampire. But he admitted to little else. His assistant—who I had no doubt also doubled as a bodyguard when necessary—stood still as a stone against the wall. Arms crossed, every time Mason's voice raised, she ran her fingers over her arm, like a smoker in great need of a cigarette. A stress response? I couldn't pull my eyes away as energy swirled and rolled around her, an ocean of menace and power. It was intoxicating and repulsive.

Mason's voice drew me back to the conversation. "So you're saying Isaiah is in Chicago?" His voice wasn't raised. If anything it had lowered. Quiet, but dangerous.

"Yes, Agent. And I'm not surprised that the OWEA hasn't discovered his arrival yet. He's quite…crafty."

Mason grunted, playing along with being underestimated. He'd mentioned the suspect being in town at lunch, but seemed to prefer that the Magister not know. He continued to question the Magister, getting an address to where the suspect was staying. My attention faltered again, and a strong hand on my shoulder brought me back to myself.

"Thank you for your time, Magister. We may have more questions, so don't make yourself scarce." He leaned toward me, his hand still on my shoulder. "Time to go," he said softly.

"Coffee?" I asked Mason when we pulled up to my town-house, even though after being around that many vampires, I wasn't going to be drinking coffee for the rest of the day. It was full dark, but not all that late. I needed to know what I'd missed in his discussion with the vampires, but couldn't think of a way to ask without sounding like an idiot. But if he came in, I might be able to get him talking.

"Okay," he said, and a spark of surprise ran through me.

I set the coffee pot to brewing and found Mason explor-ing my living room. He didn't look impressed. I frowned. My townhouse might not be anything fancy, certainly nothing like his house. But I'd paid for it out of my own pocket. It was mine. I had my doubts as to how he'd paid for his. If he'd earned it, he was somehow making a good deal more than a cop's salary.

"Is there a problem?" I asked. Then I mentally chided myself for the annoyance in my tone.

"No," he said simply. Then, without invitation, he sat on my couch.

I pushed down the irritation spiking through me and sat down on the loveseat across from him. My coffee table sat between us, and a fireplace—my biggest reason for buying the townhouse—decorated the far wall. I loved the fireplace, but more for the feeling of home it gave me than for any reduction in my heating bill.

"No television?"

I started. Is that what had disturbed him about my home? "I have a small set in my office."

He nodded and awkwardness settled over us.

"So...the conversation with the vampires was interesting," I said.

"Was it?" He raised an eyebrow at me.

Crap. My inattention must have been obvious.

"I'm curious, Detective. How do you investigate crimes when you can't even focus when questioning witnesses?"

Heat flooded my face and my ears burned. "I do just fine."

"Yes. With an investigator of Claude Desmarais's caliber leading the way, I suppose you do."

"You don't know what the—" My mother's training kicked in and I broke off before the curse word escaped my lips. "You haven't the slightest idea of what you're talking about."

"Educate me."

"Why should I?" I practically jumped up off the loveseat. "Maybe you should just go."

He didn't move from his seat.

"I'm not having an unknown factor in this investigation. Tell me or you can stay out of it."

I gaped at him. "But—"

"I don't care if you can lead me to the killer like a bloodhound," he growled. "If you can't be honest and straightforward with me then you can just stay out of it. I won't have a wildcard mucking up my case."

I sat heavily on the loveseat and took a deep breath. He was right. He had no reason to trust me, especially with how out of focus I'd been at the Magister's.

"Just tell me, Astrid."

"Have you ever worked closely with a sensitive before?"

"No. I've been around you, of course." His eyes flashed toward me and for a second all I could think about was the heat of his mouth against mine. A year had passed, but I could still feel him vividly. "I haven't been with the OWEA long enough to work with any of their sensitives."

"I'm guessing that none of them are actual investigators."

He thought about that. "I suppose not."

"I've never met another sensitive in an investigator role either."

He leaned forward, elbows on his knees and his eyes held mine. "I'm listening."

"Being a sensitive is like having a sixth sense. Except instead of it being one type of sense—like seeing or smelling or touching or hearing—it kind of meshes into a sensation that combines them."

He nodded. "Yes. I understand that."

I almost snorted. Understood it? Not likely. Not in a real way or he wouldn't have to ask about my lack of focus around otherworlders.

I got up from the loveseat again and walked around to sit next to him. A foot of couch sat between us, and I had the sudden urge to close the gap. "Close your eyes," I said instead.

His brows pinched in confusion, but he closed his eyes.

"Imagine that you're watching a movie," I murmured.

"Big screen?" he asked, voice husky.

I smiled. "Sure."

"Got it."

"Now as you're watching, a song starts to play. It's loud, and contradictory to the tone of the movie. You can still hear the movie, but you have to focus on it so you don't miss bits."

He grimaced. "Okay."

I touched his arm, my hand soft against the material of his shirt, and his power caressed my skin. Hard muscle beneath the cotton flexed in surprise at my touch, but he didn't pull away.

"Now, you're still watching your movie. The song is still sounding, but now something is touching you. Here and there. Small brushes. Barely noticeable."

A muscle in his jaw clenched and I watched it with some interest. Did my presence make him tense, or was he merely impatient?

I gripped his arm. "Now colors occasionally flash across your vision. On the screen, between the screen and you. Not enough to block your view. They're like shadows, and only if you concentrate on them can you really see them. See their form. Again, they don't interrupt your movie, but they're distracting." I dropped my hand from his arm, unable to resist a small caress as I let it fall. "And to top it all off, a smell overwhelms you—maybe burnt coffee, maybe something else. A taste invades your mouth. Maybe it's pleasant, like strawberries, but it's still uninvited."

"Coffee?"

"It's not like any creature really tastes or smells like coffee or fresh air or anything else. Energy is just energy. But the subtle differences that I can feel are interpreted by my brain. So, it interprets them in mostly familiar ways."

His eyes opened and focused on me. Shivers rushed up my spine and my breath caught in my throat. I'd expected an expression of understanding, but his face flashed with lust so plain I felt my own body clench in response.

Mason shook himself suddenly, like I imagined the beast

part of him did naturally. And when his eyes reopened, his expression was back to normal. Controlled. Violence dancing just under the surface.

"That's what you deal with all the time?" His voice had lowered to something nearing a growl.

"Not always. Usually I can tune it out. But that's what it was like to be in a room full of powerful vamps and an equally powerful lycan."

"I'm sorry I called you unfocused. Damn, Astrid." He ran his hand through his hair. "You've got to be focused as hell to act halfway normal most of the time."

My chest pinched. Halfway normal? Was that how I acted? My throat burned and I got up from the couch and turned away from him. "Look, maybe we should just call it a night, okay?" The cheer in my voice sounded false, but there wasn't a thing I could do about it.

"Astrid—"

"Please." I walked toward the kitchen, afraid I'd cry if I looked at him and saw pity in his eyes. But even more afraid of running away from him. I could still get out of this with a bit of dignity if he would just leave. I was overreacting, but I couldn't seem to help myself. I didn't want Mason, of all people, to think I was some pitiful freak who didn't fit in. I didn't want him to think of me as odd.

I wanted him to think that I was beautiful and smart and skilled. I didn't care what a lot of my coworkers thought— not that I wasn't irritated by their reactions sometimes. But they didn't matter.

Mason mattered.

I stopped at the sink and stared into my backyard. Moonlight peeked through the heavy cloud cover and reflected off of the snow that enveloped every surface. Half full.

Less than a minute later, I heard the front door open and shut. A ragged breath escaped me, and I swallowed down my tears.

Chapter Five

"So why aren't we meeting with the prime suspect right now?" I asked as we pulled up in front of a mortuary. I rubbed my arms. Even in the car with my coat on, the chill of the bright, sunny morning cut through me.

"They're having services for Jake Stone this morning." Mason cranked the heat.

I whistled under my breath. "That was fast."

"Can't let vampire bodies sit. Besides, autopsy's complete."

Of course. Vampires were unusual in that they didn't always stay dead. A truly dead vampire didn't come back—not really. But their bodies didn't always die all the way either, even when decapitated. And a zombie vampire could be messy as hell to deal with. Especially one that had been murdered. While they didn't retain much of their old selves, ones who died violently tended to act in kind. To ensure they didn't come back as killing machines, vampires had to be cremated within a few days of death.

"I get why we're here. But if the suspect leaves town while we're watching the vic's wife grieve—"

"Crafty as the Magister thinks he is, Isaiah's not the type to hide. If he leaves town, we'll be able to track him." Giving me a sidelong glance, he turned the heat up another click. "Besides, we don't have anything substantial on him. Can't hurt to take a few more hours to see if we can come up with anything."

I relaxed as the heat filled the SUV and melted into my coat. A few people trickled in for the services. I recognized Mary Stone, arriving with an equally beautiful older woman who had to be her mother.

"Our prime suspect, Isaiah, is around two hundred and fifty years old according to Luc Chevalier. That matches what the OWEA has been able to dig up." Mason took a sip of his Starbucks.

"And the Magister thinks he's responsible?" I kept my voice even, but I wanted to reach out and give Mason a big kiss on the cheek for passing along the information I'd missed the night before without making a big deal about it.

"He strongly suspects him."

"I'm surprised that the Magister hasn't taken care of it himself," I murmured.

"Oh I'm well aware of the vampires' tendency to take care of their own business. But the OWEA is already aware of this guy. Besides, Luc isn't likely to take out someone he might want to hire himself someday."

I started at the thought. But of course it wouldn't be personal to the Magister. He might want vengeance on whoever hired the hitter, but not on the hitter himself. Jake Stone wasn't a personal friend or family member of the Magister's.

If it had been someone like Nicolas, I had no doubt that Luc Chevalier would have been unstoppable in his vengeance.

Guests filed into the mortuary, fewer than I would have expected. But then, Jake Stone wasn't from Chicago, and it was entirely possible that not all of his friends and family could make the trip on such short notice.

"I'm going to go speak to the suspect alone later this afternoon," Mason said after the parking lot had quieted.

"Pardon?" I turned in my seat to face him.

He sipped his coffee, not at all ruffled by my tone. "I don't think it's a good idea for you to go."

"Why?" I said flatly.

"It's not safe."

"I'm sick and tired of people thinking I'm made of glass or something. Granted, I don't have any offensive abilities, but a lot of normal cops don't, and they manage just fine. I have a personal sidearm." I didn't add that it was still in the glove box of my car. He could see for himself that I wasn't carrying at the moment. "And I know how to use it."

"Not much help against a vampire. Besides, do you even have a permit to carry concealed as a citizen, not a cop?"

"Vampires will go down if you get enough bullets into them," I countered, ignoring his permit question. I'd never needed a permit before, so of course I didn't have one. But I viewed that as a technicality. I'd get my badge back, and his point would be moot.

Mason nodded. "Sure they will. If you can get one to hold still long enough to shoot him."

"I'm going with you. This case is more important than your overprotective machismo bullshit." I clapped my hand over my mouth and Mason let out a short laugh at my expression.

"Cussing isn't against the law. You know that, right?"

I ignored his silly question and the heat bathing my face. "It's important for me to go."

He glanced down at his coffee before returning his gaze to me. "Your safety is more important." His voice was so soft that I thought I'd misheard him, but there was no escaping the flash of emotion on his face.

Mason Sanderson cared about me.

My breath caught and my heart thundered in my chest. I almost wanted to give in. Almost. If only to give this handsome man what he wanted. If only to revel in the fact that he had feelings for me. If only to let someone take care of me, even just for a minute.

But I couldn't do that. My pride wouldn't let me, and neither would my good sense. I was an adult, not some kid looking for someone to worry about her. And Mason had made his feelings clear the year before. Even if it seemed like he cared for me, he didn't care for me in any lasting way. Not enough to want me in his life.

"What if he's the coin's owner?" I asked. Another lie hiding as an omission. Guilt pressed against my mind, rising from my heart. If all the otherworlder auras didn't give me a blasted migraine during this case, the guilt certainly would.

He tensed then rubbed his face with his hands. "Fuck. You're right. You can't very well ID him if you aren't there."

I nodded and gave him a half-smile. He returned the expression with a sardonic grin. The look was so rare for him it shot straight through me. I swallowed hard and tore my eyes away to watch the mortuary, fearing if I looked at him for one more second I'd blurt out the truth.

Perhaps sensing my change in mood, Mason watched the mortuary silently.

We sipped our coffee and shared some beef jerky that Mason carried in his glove compartment. Not my snack of choice, but the lycan seemed to enjoy it. Finally, the funeral service ended and people began filing out two and three at a time. Even from across the street I could feel several different species of oh-dubs, mainly vampires. But at this distance, they sort of melded together and the energy was weaker. It made it easier for me to concentrate, but it also meant I was surprised when Nicolas Chevalier walked out, holding Mary Stone's arm and supporting her weight as she leaned against him.

"What's he doing here?"

Mason shrugged. "Probably a polite vampire thing. Guessing he's here to represent Luc."

"I suppose." But something about the way the vampire held the succubus's arm didn't sit right with me. Mary seemed stiff and uncomfortable, but that could very well be because she was at her husband's funeral.

The SUV roared to life and I jumped a little. "Are we going to the cemetery, too?" My stomach let out a loud noise, its vote obvious.

Mason snorted. "Let's get some lunch and then go talk to Isaiah. I don't think we're going to find out much more here. Waste of time."

"Perhaps," I said, and glanced out the window to the spot where Nicolas Chevalier and the widow had stood. I wasn't convinced that there was no value in our trip.

Despite the chill breeze whipping its way through the city, and the snow and ice covering the ground, Mason suggested that we eat from a hot dog vendor–outside. Seeing the perspiration touching his brow after he had kept the car temperature high enough for me to be comfortable all morning, I agreed.

We drove down to the city, exchanging a few words during the trip. I half expected him to change his mind again and decide that I shouldn't come along with him to question Isaiah, and I didn't want to tip the unsteady balance between us. So I stayed quiet.

Mason parked in an underground parking garage on Michigan Avenue and we snagged hotdogs from a vendor a short walk away. With my hat and gloves on, and my coat pulled tight around my body, the cold wasn't too difficult to bear. Finding an unoccupied bench near the hotdog vendor, we sat and munched on our dogs, eager to finish them before they froze.

I watched Mason as I chewed my food. His posture was relaxed and his face more open than I was used to seeing on him. "You don't care to be indoors all the time, do you?" I asked.

He shrugged. "I suppose it's a lycan thing. Half-beasts like to be under the sky."

"I'm surprised that you don't live farther out in the burbs. With land or something." I popped the last bite of hotdog into my mouth and then crumpled the wrapper into a small ball.

"I like commutes even less than a lack of space. Besides, my home is my place." He gave me a tight smile. "My territory, you could say. I don't feel as uncomfortable there."

A snicker escaped me as the image of Mason rubbing all over his furniture to claim it flashed in my mind.

"What?" he asked, amused.

"Nothing."

He raised an eyebrow.

"Really. You don't want to know." The idea was ludicrous. Mason wasn't that much of a beast. Besides, I wasn't even sure a wolf would mark their scents the same way my cat seemed to. Heck, wolves probably…oh goodness, no. He couldn't.

Mason watched my expression in fascination as I tried to decide whether a lycan would mark his territory like a domestic dog. Finally I threw an arm over my face dramatically. "Quit looking at me or I'll have to tell you what I was thinking, and you'll never think well of me again."

Mason let out a small noise that sounded suspiciously like a chuckle, but when I dropped my arm to my side, his expression was back to normal.

"When we talk to Isaiah, you're going to need to try to keep your thoughts off your face, Astrid."

My smile faltered. "I know."

"I'm serious. If you show how much you know and he's our guy, he'll pick up on it—hell even if he isn't our guy in this case, I don't want him to know we're aware of that."

I brushed at my nose, which was now almost numb from the cold around us. Cold that I hadn't even noticed when I had been distracted by Mason's good humor. But now that professional Mason was back, I felt everything more sharply. I pushed up from the bench. "I get that this is serious, Mason. I'm not a child. And this isn't my first investigation."

"All right, then."

"All right," I echoed. "Let's get going. I'm sick of the cold." How could he switch it on and off like that? Humorous and almost normal one second, and cold and gruff the next? And I was fully aware of the necessity of keeping my feelings hidden around a suspect, especially a vampire with a reputation like Isaiah's.

I made it a few steps away before the anger pulsing in me had to find an outlet. "I might not have the best poker face in the world, but we're none of us perfect."

"No, we aren't."

I narrowed my eyes. I wasn't ready for his platitudes when embarrassment still surged through me. "Speaking of which, you intimidate everyone around you. I want to speak to the wife alone. I think she might be more inclined to confide in me if you're not there glowering at her."

"That's not a good idea." He crossed his arms.

I poked at his chest, ignoring the rush I got from the simple touch. "The succubus isn't going to jump me. And if you're paranoid about it, you can wait in the car. Like a good boy."

His mouth dropped open and I couldn't help but notice how *not* intimidating he looked with an expression of shock on his face. And despite the ridiculousness of my comment, I had a hard time suppressing a laugh. A second later, he snapped his mouth shut. Pushing my chin into the air, I waited for his comeback. Finally, he said, "Fine."

Not bothering to keep the triumph I felt at the small win off my face, I nodded and continued down the sidewalk.

Mason and I walked to the swanky hotel where the suspected vampire assassin was staying while he was in the Chicago area. It struck me as odd that he wasn't hiding out in a dank hole somewhere, but I guessed there was no accounting for vampire politics and behavior.

We rode the elevator in silence, but Mason's posture had straightened, and his fists clenched tighter at his sides the closer we got. I doubted my heart pounding nervously in my chest was good for his nerves, not to mention that I'd suddenly started sweating. Probably not something I'd normally notice, but knowing how good Mason's sense of smell was made me conscious of it.

The elevator pinged open, and for once Mason violated his ladies first mindset and stepped out in front of me. I exited the elevator behind him. He paused and turned to me, then touched my shoulder softly, before continuing down the hall. Confidence seemed to flow from his hand, and some of my worry melted away. I was suddenly certain that the lycan beside me could handle whatever threat the vampire might offer. True or not, the thought made me feel better.

I stood back while Mason knocked on the door and then confronted its occupant. From my position next to the door, I was unable to see the man who answered, but I could feel him.

Isaiah's voice was low-pitched and smooth, and when he invited us in, I paused for a second to examine him. Dark skin covered a large, well-muscled frame that would no doubt have women drooling if it wasn't for the aura of fear surrounding him. As it was, with my enhanced senses, his energy was almost stifling to my regular vision and burnt coffee already clung to my nose. But he exuded confidence and violence, and I decided that he probably had no trouble with women—intimidating aura or no.

"I'm confused as to why you're here to see me, Agent," Isaiah said.

"When did you get into town, Isaiah?" Mason asked, ignoring the vampire's question.

The hotel suite was nicely decorated, with a half-wall partially blocking our view of the large king-sized bed behind it. A couch and large television occupied our area, as well as a small desk and office chair. Isaiah did not invite us to sit down.

"A week, I suppose," the vampire replied.

"And what brings you to Chicago?"

"None of your business."

Mason smiled, and the look was predatory and grim. "We can discuss this downtown if you'd prefer."

The vampire returned the smile, perfect white teeth flashing. I caught a glimpse of fang. "That won't be necessary, I'm sure. I'm here on business."

"What sort of business," Mason shot back.

"The private kind," Isaiah said, voice still full of good humor. The vampire, it would seem, was not easy to anger. A good quality, I supposed, in a professional killer.

The conversation faded around me as I focused more closely on my other senses. Isaiah's power proved as staggering as I'd expected. And I had the sudden urge to put him in a room with the Magister just so I could determine who was more powerful.

I closed my eyes as his aura rolled around me, and I could hear the voices that had faded to murmurs, pause. Mason touched my shoulder. I glanced at him and there were questions in his eyes. "I'm fine," I muttered, and then I closed my eyes again. Not something I'd normally do with a powerful vampire assassin in the room with me, but I trusted Mason to keep me safe.

I only knew one other vampire who I'd match against Luc—and I knew that Claude had his own reasons for staying in Chicago and serving the Magister. But I wondered why Isaiah didn't run his own little vampire world somewhere. A certain amount of vampire standing was gained through politicking, but much could be gained with pure brute strength.

And Isaiah had plenty of it.

I took a deep breath and wiped my brow against the arm of my jacket. Sweat coated my forehead and built between my breasts and down my back. A consequence of ignoring my body's order to run from Isaiah's aura of fear.

Could Isaiah be the owner of the coin that had gone missing from evidence? He certainly possessed the power to so fully coat the coin, but then, most vampires could have done the same if they had held onto it long enough. Nothing about his aura was particularly familiar, but that didn't mean much. Despite what I'd told Mason, I couldn't identify the killer from that power signature. It hadn't really felt any more specific than a vampire who carried a hefty fear aura.

I wanted to yell in frustration. I'd hoped for his signature to be familiar, at least. It would give me something to tell Mason, something to make my lie into the truth.

But I had zilch. And after tonight, Mason was going to know I'd lied.

"I've heard that you've had a bit of trouble holding on to your evidence," Isaiah was saying as I picked back up on the conversation. He smiled at me, and my stomach clenched and my breath came faster. It took everything I had not to back out into the hall and run away from the vampire in front of me. The smile was like that of a shark, and it disappeared quickly.

Mason stiffened and took a single short step to his side, placing himself slightly between Isaiah and me. "I'm sure we don't know what you're talking about," Mason said, a warning in his voice.

Isaiah continued, as if he hadn't noticed the tension the lycan now emanated. "An unfortunate loss, that coin."

"What do you know about it?" Mason asked.

I forced my expression to stay even, but I almost started at Mason's admission. But pretending the coin didn't exist wouldn't get us anywhere. The vampire obviously had sources of information, either with the police or more likely in the local vamp community.

Isaiah's gaze flashed to me before returning to Mason. "I've heard things—rumors. Managing things so recklessly, you're lucky no one has gotten hurt." A slight grin touched his lips. "Then again, your investigation is still young. And I suppose accidents are inevitable in your line of work." Again, his gaze slid to me. It was subtle, but the threat was as clear as if he'd slid his finger across his throat, in a macabre imitation of a knife.

Mason shoved Isaiah against the wall, his forearm under the vampire's neck, and their faces only inches apart. I blinked at them before reaching for my gun. I'd known that lycans were fast—even in their fully human form—but I hadn't known they were *that* fast.

"Was that some kind of fucking threat, you undead piece

of shit?" Mason's hard voice was low and controlled, despite his words. "Because you look at her again with a threat on your tongue and I will rip your fucking head off."

I gaped at his words, and my hand found nothing. Shit. I didn't have a sidearm. Great. All I could do was stand and stare and pretend that I had a holster on my back. Doing my best to smooth my expression, I hoped I looked convincingly unaffected and ready to pull my weapon at any second.

But neither man seemed to remember I was in the room, and as the seconds ticked by, the tension was so thick it choked me. The power rolled off them, mixing with the violence to create a room set to explode.

I couldn't think about what Mason had said and what it might mean, but the possibilities kicked my heart rate up a notch. And looking at the dead, deep eyes of the vampire, the professional killer who had murdered his own kind for years, I wasn't entirely sure which side would come out on top if it came down to it.

I had to diffuse the anger, before the balance tipped. "Thank you for answering our questions, Isaiah," I said in the most civil and disinterested voice I could manage. "We'll be in touch. It would be best if you didn't leave town for a few days."

Like the fuse fizzling out on a bomb, the tension dissipated, and Mason released the vampire.

Chapter Six

"Well?" Mason asked when we were safely in his SUV.

"Can we talk when we get to my place, please?" I rubbed my temples and wished that I was just asking in order to postpone the inevitable, but the power and menace rolling off of that vamp had been overwhelming, especially with Mason's energy jockeying for my attention. Trying to push it away to actually pay attention to the conversation and then jump back into the swirl in the inane hope of matching Isaiah to the coin had given me a splitting headache.

"Sure," Mason said.

"And I'm bringing my personal sidearm from now on." If Mason wasn't going to bring up the close call we'd just had, neither was I. But I'd be damned if I'd go in to question a suspect like Isaiah without a gun again. Legality be damned.

Mason grunted his agreement.

I pulled a small bottle of Advil from my purse and tossed a couple in my mouth. I chewed them, an old trick to make them work faster, but the taste made me grimace. Part of me wanted to ask if his reaction to what he perceived as a threat against me from Isaiah meant anything. But how did I start the conversation? And what if he would have done the same for any coworker who'd been standing in my place? The whole thing made my head pound harder.

"There's a bottle of water in there." Mason nodded toward the glove box. "It's old, but unopened, so it should still be okay."

I flipped down the glove box door and grabbed the water. I swallowed the remnants of the pills with a large gulp, thankful I didn't have to choke them down dry.

"Thanks," I said after I'd dislodged the crushed pieces of the pills from my throat.

"Sure."

We drove to my townhouse in silence. Mason parked on the street in front of my building and followed me up the sidewalk to my house. But he stopped in the doorway. I turned to see his face scrunched in concentration.

"What is it?" I asked, glancing around my foyer. Nothing appeared disturbed.

"Your cat never comes out to say hello." He shut the door.

My headache had started to fade—probably more from the time away from Isaiah's energy than from the Advil kicking in—which left me in an almost good mood from the relief. I grinned. "Yes well, I'm sure he doesn't particularly want to meet you. His name is Charlie. And this is his house more than mine, so you'll have to show him some respect."

"Respectable people have dogs, you know," he informed me as we walked to the kitchen.

"Do they? Guess I'm not respectable."

He just snorted and sat at my small eat-in table.

"Want something to drink?" I asked, suddenly nervous again. I couldn't put this conversation off. There was no way to avoid Mason finding out that I'd been dishonest without lying further. And I couldn't lie about Isaiah's signature. If I said it was his coin, the vampire could get in trouble for something he may not have done—his past history as an assassin notwithstanding. Besides, that kind of deceit would be so morally wrong that just thinking about it made my stomach turn.

And I couldn't tell Mason that I didn't recognize Isaiah's aura and still pretend that I could ID the vamp off of the coin. That would make Mason think that Isaiah definitely wasn't responsible, which he might very well be.

I'd backed myself into a corner.

I opened my refrigerator and peered inside. "I've got orange juice and Coke. Or beer."

"Beer, please."

Of course. I grabbed a Heineken and a Coke and poured them into glasses, avoiding Mason as long as I could.

"What's wrong, Astrid?" Mason asked.

I set his drink down and then sat in the seat next to him. His face had softened, and his concern was apparent. Crap. Of course he'd look at me like that right before he was going to be out of my life for good.

I drank a swallow of my Coke and for once wished it had something alcoholic in it. "I don't know if Isaiah is the killer. I can't tell." I kept my eyes firmly affixed to the glass and tensed in preparation for the explosion I knew was coming.

Mason sipped his beer and didn't say anything for a few

seconds. When he spoke, his voice was low, but something in the air had changed. Electrified. "Because you can't get as good a read as you thought you'd be able to, or because you knew you'd never be able to ID the killer from what you felt on that coin?"

It was a question we both already knew the answer to, and it hurt my heart that he thought enough of me to even consider the other possibility. Part of me wanted to take the out he'd given me. But I'd lied enough. "I can't ID the owner off the aura I felt on the coin. It wasn't distinct enough."

"And you knew that from the beginning?" he growled.

I steeled my spine and met his gaze. "Yes."

"So you lied to my face."

"I omitted."

"You omitted?" His voice rose, harsh against my ears.

I jutted my chin out. "I never actually said—"

"The hell you didn't! Near enough."

"I'm sorry, okay? You're right. I lied. I deceived you on purpose. And maybe that makes me a total bitch but I don't care." *Talk like a lady or no one will treat you like one.* Like my mother's rules mattered now. I was a liar, and deserved every bit of Mason's ire.

"You don't care?" He asked. His voice returned to a low growl, but somehow sounded even more dangerous. And filled with more anger.

"It's my badge on the line! I had to be in on the investigation."

He stared at me for a second, intense gaze never leaving my own, then he shook his head.

"I didn't have a choice." My voice thinned and I swallowed hard, dangerously close to tears. I didn't, did I?

No. I'd had to have at least some control over this. Some control over keeping my job.

"You could have told me the truth." Voice flat, he seemed deflated. As if the anger had drained out of him.

"You wouldn't have let me in," I insisted. Would he? Even the possibility hadn't occurred to me. Why would he?

He barked out a short laugh and dropped his eyes to his glass. "You don't have any fucking idea what I'd do for you."

My mouth dropped open, and before I could think of anything to say, he pushed up from the table and left.

Snow fell silently outside of my bedroom, adding to the ten-inch pile already on the balcony. I rolled over, pulling my down comforter closer around my neck, and met Charlie's unblinking eyes.

I reached out and scratched his chin, and the bit of light leaking from the sliding glass doors reflected off of his black fur. "Think I messed up big time, buddy."

Charlie yawned and his eyes closed. I sat up and glanced at the clock. One fifteen. Great. The way I was going, I'd be up the rest of the night.

Mason's words reverberated through my mind, and despite my best efforts to sleep, my brain insisted on examining each and every potential meaning behind them. And for once, I wished for the familiarity of my mother's voice in my head, instead of the foreignness of his voice and intent.

You don't have any fucking idea what I'd do for you.

What the hell was that supposed to mean? If he cared about me, why couldn't he just say it? Why had he called our kiss a mistake, and why had he avoided me ever since? The words seemed to mean that he cared about me. A lot. But that was tough to wrap my mind around. And I was scared to think about it too much. Scared to hope. What if I was wrong? What if he meant something else entirely by those words, something more akin to the loyalty shared by cops, not the caring shared by lovers. I couldn't take the chance. If my own family couldn't—no, I wasn't going there. Sure, he'd kissed me. But only once. A year ago.

Oh there'd been looks before that. Times when I would feel his gaze burning into me. But when I'd turn to look at him, his eyes would be elsewhere. I'd convinced myself that I'd imagined his interest. And we had talked, but it had been just friendly chatting. Granted, I hadn't noticed Mason talking to others in such an easy manner, but I'd always figured it was because—unlike most of the tough macho cops I worked with—I was quiet, and maybe easier to talk to. I'd thought that simple friendliness was all it was.

Until that night.

Two days before Christmas. I'd gone outside to get a breather from the mostly oh-dub crowd at the party. Snow had covered the ground, so similar to what the outside looked like right now. His gaze had been hot against my back. I'd whipped my head around to stare at him. His eyes had reflected the moonlight that bounced up off the snow in a way only a lycan's could and he'd closed the gap between us without a word.

Then he had kissed me.

I'd lost a bit of myself in that kiss. Maybe Mason had too.

I closed my eyes and tried to relax, firmly banishing thoughts of him from my mind. My hand slid down Charlie's fur, and the cat leaned against me. I could feel vampiric energy faintly, like seeing a flash in my peripheral vision. For a moment, I thought I'd fallen into a dream. But as Charlie purred loudly my eyes flew open.

A soft scratching sound touched my ears faintly. My stomach dropped. Someone picking the lock?

I hadn't dreamed the vampiric energy; it was still there, on the edge of my ability to feel it. The slightest smell of burnt coffee, and shadows lurking just beyond where I could see them. If I stayed put a few more seconds, let them get closer, I might be able to determine who the vampire was. If it was one I'd met before. But if whoever was scratching at my lock got through my door, once they got in they'd be too fast for me to escape. I wouldn't have enough time to get away.

And like a prize idiot, I'd left my gun downstairs in my car.

Charlie jumped off the bed and pattered down the hall. I opened my mouth to hiss at him to come back, but snapped it shut before a sound could escape.

A vampire would hear such a sound. Maybe. I couldn't chance it. Charlie wasn't one to obey orders regardless. And if I pursued him, I would undoubtedly be caught. Charlie would probably be fine. My intruder wouldn't be interested in a pet. *I* would not be so lucky.

Blinking back tears at the thought of them hurting Charlie, I gave the room one last desperate glance before I opened the sliding glass door that led to my balcony.

Stay hidden, I told the cat silently.

The cold air bit into my skin, which was protected only by a T-shirt and cotton shorts. The door slid quietly behind me, and I heard the click of my front door opening a split second before the sliding glass moved into place.

The first two feet of the balcony from the house were free of most of the snow piling the last foot or so, protected by a short awning in the roof. Wincing, I walked barefoot into the crisply-edged snow and stepped over the balcony. The edge was only a couple of inches between the banister and the gaping darkness to my backyard below. My toes were on fire, and I knew I'd have only minutes before they would numb. I held onto the top of the balcony with one hand and then bent down and gripped the bottom of the railing with the other. I slid my hand from the top down to grip the railing next to my other hand.

Freezing air rushed into my lungs when I took a deep breath. Was the vampire getting closer? I didn't dare drop my concentration from what I was doing to feel out with my senses. Had he or she seen me yet? I didn't risk a glance at the sliding glass door. Instead, I slid one foot, then the next off the railing, wincing as the wood scraped at my legs and arms. Dangling, I knew I was likely to hurt myself—even dropping from only the second story while already hanging several feet closer to the ground. But I didn't have a choice.

I released the railing and fire bit at my inner arms as they slid against the wood. I hit the ground, crunching the snow beneath my feet. Shock rushed up through my ankles and knees. Then I slid, my feet rushed out from under me and I fell to my butt with a *whump*.

Coldness surrounded me. Panic coursed through me. Had I cried out when I hit the ground? I thought I might have. The walls in my townhouse were thick, and with the doors shut and the noise of a train passing, I hoped the vampire hadn't heard me.

I forced myself up, thankful that the bit of snow on the ground had at least cushioned me a little, and rushed to the fence. Nothing seemed broken, and while I could feel a slight ache from my ankle, the adrenaline running through me pushed it all to the back of my awareness.

The privacy fence cut into my hands when I pulled myself over it and dropped onto the street behind my home. Where to? My mind rebelled at offering any logical location to run to, it was as if I'd forgotten the layout of my own neighborhood.

I loped toward the main street running alongside my subdivision and tried to breathe. My brain finally slowed enough for me to think. A neighbor's house wouldn't work. That would just put them in danger. Somewhere public and well lit would be better. The 7-11 right down the street was open twenty-four hours. I'd head there.

Somewhere along the quarter mile between me and the convenience store, my aches started to press their way through the adrenaline. My right ankle was the worst. It pulsed painfully with every heartbeat. And the cold made my whole body shiver and shake, slowing my progress.

But I couldn't feel a vampire behind me. And I clung to that knowledge, and the bit of hope it offered. Finally, after what felt like hours—but was probably only minutes later— I found myself blinking at the bright lights of the 7-11. My haven. I trotted up to the front doors and shoved them open.

A clerk stared at me, jaw dropping. Young, she couldn't have been far out of high school. What was she doing working the graveyard shift alone?

"Lock the front door," I told her. When she didn't move, I yelled, "I'm a cop. Lock that door immediately. We could both be in danger. Where's your phone?"

My words were stilted, I couldn't seem to talk right through the cold, but the authority in my tone, or maybe the word *cop*, pulled her out of her shock. She grabbed a cordless phone out from under the counter and handed it to me. Then the girl shuffled to the front door, hands shakily searching through a key ring while I dialed 911.

I told the operator my name and badge number, and that I needed backup at the store. Then I told her we might be dealing with a dangerous vampire and hung up the phone before she could ask more questions.

I called Mason next, and the gravelly tone of his voice made me wonder if he'd had trouble sleeping too, before I could pull my mind back to why I was calling.

"Mason, it's me."

"Astrid. Do you know what time it is?" Anger coated his tone, and I swallowed my guilt.

"Look," I said before he could hang up on me. "A vamp broke into my townhouse tonight. I got out, but I'd appreciate it if you'd come down here." To my horror, I realized that my voice was higher pitched than normal, and wispy thin, on the edge of breaking. I couldn't cry right now. I had to be strong. For the clerk who still watched me with wide eyes, at least.

"Where are you?" he asked, all trace of sleepiness gone from his tone.

I told him, and then I clung to the phone. He didn't hang up, though he put the phone down for a few seconds to toss a coat on. I heard his SUV fire up and I watched the door warily.

The clerk wrapped a small, fuzzy blanket around my shoulders. It still had a price tag clinging to it. Mason and I didn't say much on the phone. Just reassured each other we were still there. Finally, red and blue flashed through the windows, and relief flooded me. I blinked back tears and tried to ignore the burning in my throat, as my brothers in blue came to my rescue.

Chapter Seven

That moment of second guessing myself—a moment that I suspect happens to many people who find themselves coming through dramatic, difficult to explain situations relatively unscathed—hit me right after I saw my brothers in arms pulling up to the 7-11.

What if I'd actually been half asleep? What if I only thought I'd sensed a vampire? What if it was all just some sort of horrible dream?

Mason arrived shortly after the first set of officers, while I was still filling them in. And I idly wondered how many red lights he'd had to run to get to my side of town so quickly.

I met his gaze, holding on to my last bit of control with the most tenuous of grips. Worry creased his brow and drew lines around his mouth. His body was tense, and his fists were clenched at his sides like he desperately wanted to hit something.

He spoke briskly with the officers who were talking

to me, taking over immediately and surprisingly with no argument from the others on scene.

Without speaking, he tugged the slight blanket off of my shoulders. Then he took off his jacket and wrapped it around me, zipping it up. The material was thicker than the blanket, and soaked in his otherworldly warmth. Then he helped me get my arms up through the sleeves, luckily the coat was large enough we managed even with the front zipped. The thing must have looked ridiculously big on me, but his eyes showed no amusement.

His gaze took in my face and then traveled to my legs and feet. He grimaced and I glanced down. No wonder the 7-11 cashier had looked at me with such shock. Blood dried on my feet, my right ankle was swollen, and long, angry scratches covered my legs and arms. When had that happened? Jumping off the balcony? Going over the old wood fence? As if spurred by seeing the injuries, pain flared in my legs and most especially from my feet. My ankle throbbed.

"You okay?" His voice was low and carefully controlled, but violence flashed behind his eyes.

I nodded, not trusting myself to speak.

He looked over me again quickly, then glanced behind him. An ambulance approached, siren sounding and lights flashing. My stomach lurched. So much drama. So many people involved. What if I'd imagined the whole thing?

Mason picked me up, cradling me against his body. I squeaked at the unexpected motion, but didn't protest. He was warm, and in his arms a feeling washed over me that I hadn't felt in a very long time. And would never have expected to feel less than an hour after jumping from my balcony to escape a vampire breaking into my home.

I felt safe.

I relaxed against him and let my head rest against his strong shoulder. As my adrenaline faded, exhaustion washed over me. And I found my mind drifting as he carried me to the ambulance.

"I should go with the officers to check out your town-house," Mason said softly as we exited the 7-11 and the chill wind whipped over us.

I shivered against him and gripped his shoulder hard. I didn't want him to go, but I couldn't seem to come up with a reason for him to stay that I could speak aloud. Don't go because I desperately need you by my side right now to feel safe? Don't go because I am afraid that I imagined the whole thing, and you'll go there and just think worse of me? Don't go because I want, more than anything in the world, to stay in your arms?

But I couldn't say any of those things, so I just clung to him.

"You're right," he said as if I'd spoken. "I'll stay with you. We'll go over after the EMT's have a look at you."

I took a deep breath, inhaling his comforting scent of soap and toothpaste and the primal smell of him beneath the other odors, and nodded against his shoulder. His grip tightened around me. Encouraging him to go would be the right thing to do, but I just couldn't force myself to pretend I didn't want him with me.

The paramedics looked over me quickly, declaring me in no danger of bleeding to death. They wanted to take me to the hospital to get my wounds treated and my ankle looked at, but I managed to convince them to do what they could and that I'd seek the hospital later. They muttered something about cops that sounded vaguely derogatory, but patched me up anyway.

Mason picked me up again after my ankle had been securely wrapped and my cuts treated and mostly bandaged. My feet were the worst off. But I was proud that I hadn't cried yet, not over the injuries or the fear, and I hadn't even cursed at the paramedics when they had disinfected the bottoms of my feet.

But oh, how I'd wanted to.

We drove the short distance to my townhouse in silence, but the tension in the air was palpable. I was worried, but Mason was something else. Something that felt to me like barely controlled rage.

We parked and Mason carried me to the front door. The officer guarding it nodded to us and let us in without us having to even flash our badges.

"Are you okay to walk?" Mason asked when we passed over my threshold.

"I'll be fine."

He set me down gingerly and watched me take a couple of steps. Satisfied I wasn't going to fall and injure myself, he strode past me into the living room. I followed more slowly, just in time to see Vasquez turn to greet Mason.

My heart dropped into my stomach at the sight of my boss. And worry made my body tense even further. But when I approached him, some of my tension faded.

"Front door lock was picked by a pro. Only very small scratches around the lock. The place doesn't look tossed, but someone tracked snow through the house. And your bedroom was a little trashed. Some pictures tossed around. Your lamp was tossed at your wall. Guess whoever broke in wasn't happy to find you weren't home."

Mason headed upstairs, no doubt to check the damage for himself.

A thought hit me, and I knelt to look under the furniture, ignoring the pain shooting up my ankle.

"Have you seen my cat?" I asked, feeling more than a little desperate.

Vasquez grunted. "Got her locked in a bathroom upstairs. She's fine. One of the officers grabbed her. Didn't think you'd want her getting out."

I opened my mouth to tell the lieutenant that Charlie was, in fact, a boy, but thought better of it. The sex of my cat was probably the last thing on Vasquez's mind.

A door slammed loudly upstairs. Vasquez put his hand on his gun. "Stay here," he said, then he took the stairs two at a time.

Ignoring the order, I followed at his heels. This was my house. No one could boss me around in my own home. And Mason was up there.

We got to the second story just in time to see Mason push away from my spare bathroom door. He glared at me, as if I'd somehow done him wrong.

"Found your cat," he said.

Vasquez snorted.

Now that things were slowing down, the implications and questions started running through my mind, and I tuned out Vasquez and Mason for a few seconds. Someone broke into my house—a vampire. And the likelihood that they were there to talk was pretty damn nonexistent. But why me? Why were they in my house?

Vasquez, echoing my own mental questions, brought my

attention back to their conversation. "What I don't under-stand is what a vamp was doing here?"

I opened my mouth to confess that I'd been working the case with Mason, and that could be why they'd come, but Mason spoke first.

"She touched that coin," Mason said. "And she's a known sensitive. Might be that the killer thinks she can identify him or her from it."

His twisting of my own lie made me grimace, even though what he said made entirely too much sense for my comfort, but Vasquez nodded thoughtfully.

"We'll put her in a safe house with protective custody until this case is solved."

"I don't think so—" I said at the exact same time Mason said, "No, she's safer with me."

I blinked at Mason, and the shock running through me was mirrored in Lieutenant Vasquez's expression.

"What do you mean, safer with you?"

"Chances are she might be able to help identify the kill-er. Keep a car on my house to help in case we need it, and I'll watch her."

"That's highly irregular," Vasquez said. He shook his head. "No, it's not worth the risk."

"She's staying with me. She's a witness in an OWEA in-vestigation and that puts her under my jurisdiction." Ma-son's voice remained low, but he bit off his words.

"Now you wait a damn minute—"

"I'm going to Mason's," I said, and both of them blinked at me. I wasn't entirely sure where the words came from, but the idea of going into protective custody, where I couldn't even help clear my name, made my stomach twist. But the thought of staying in my own house, which had until such a short time before felt so safe, pushed panic up into my throat.

"I don't think that's—" Vasquez began.

"She's said what she wants," Mason cut in.

"Stop arguing, both of you," I said as Vasquez opened his mouth. "I'm not going under protective custody. I'm under administrative leave, right? At least until my badge is taken from me permanently." I turned slightly to stare down Mason. "I'm under no one's jurisdiction, and I'll thank you to remember that. I'll stay with you because it's what I want to do, not because I fall under your command." I stood straighter. "And if you two care to argue about it anymore you can do it outside." I pointed to the door.

I watched Mason bravely go into the bathroom to retrieve my cat, while I held the carrier. Mason carried Charlie like a bomb, as far from his body as possible, while Charlie glared daggers and struggled to get free. Charlie wasn't terribly excited to be carted around in his carrier by a lycan, and Mason looked positively disgusted when I placed the cat's litter box in a spare bathroom adjacent to my room at Mason's. After getting Charlie settled, I walked back down to Mason's living room.

My feet were still sore, even with the mountain of aspirin I'd consumed. Driving my own car hadn't helped, but I didn't want to be without it. No transportation would make me feel just a little trapped. I'd elected to go straight to Mason's instead of hitting the hospital first. My ankle was only twisted, and I reassured Mason that if the swelling didn't go down I would go to the doctor's office later.

"Got you some ice," Mason said, holding out an ice pack.

"Thanks." I grimaced. I'd found a new level of hatred for ice, but if it kept me from the doctor's it would be worth the discomfort.

"You should go to bed. Rest for a few hours."

"Soon. I just need to relax for a while first." Preferably not alone, but I didn't dare say that.

I sat in a corner of the couch and propped my foot up. Mason gently placed my foot on his lap and then carefully wrapped it with the ice pack. The whole situation was comfortable — too comfortable. I glanced around the living room and tried to ignore the cold sinking into my skin. Warmly decorated, but with no pets or other people, the house felt awfully lonely.

"Looking for something?"

"Just seems like such a large place for one guy."

"Suits me fine."

"I'm sure it does, but still strikes me as kind of lonely."

"I'm not lonely," he growled.

I raised my eyebrows at him and ignored the voice in my head telling me to be polite and leave it alone. "Oh, did I touch a nerve?"

"No."

I tugged on a chunk of my hair and finally blurted out exactly what was on my mind. "Are you going to hold that small omission against me forever?"

"Small omission? You lied to me. Point blank. Didn't even give me the chance to — "

"Oh, I gave you a chance, all right. But it was obvious

that you weren't going to take it."

"Was it? Well a lie is still a lie."

"I'm not the only one who hasn't been entirely honest." I pulled my foot away from him and sat up straight on the couch, balancing so the ice pack stayed on as I set my foot on the floor. I didn't quite have it in me to stand up, but I wasn't going to argue lying down either.

"Why did you kiss me last year?" I asked. The timing couldn't have possibly been worse. After I'd lied to him and he'd been forced to take me in. But if I hadn't been awake, tossing and turning with thoughts of Mason troubling my mind, I wouldn't have sensed that vampire and who knows what would have happened? And for some reason, that loosened my tongue.

He drew back as if I'd struck him, then his face hardened even further. "Because I wanted to."

At least he hadn't said because he had drunk too much. "Always honest, huh? You kiss me, then you call it a mistake. You act like you care about me one minute, then like you couldn't care less the next. You say things like...like what you said earlier tonight, and then you act like a stranger."

"I've never lied to you."

"Didn't you?" My voice raised and for once I didn't try to stifle my anger. I'd lost too many hours of sleep over the man. "You lied when you said that kiss was a mistake and then followed me with your eyes for months after. You lied when you just said you kissed me because you felt like it in the moment." I leaned closer to him with every word until we were only inches apart. "Why?"

I had only a split second of warning before his mouth fell onto mine. Hard and without allowing any recourse, his lips pressed against me. Someone made a small noise, needy. It might have been me.

Emotion and lust rushed through me and I opened my mouth to him. His tongue stroked mine, leaving heat and need in its wake. And he growled low in his throat.

The constant worry about my job, about Mason, about my family, all faded into the background. There was only him. His masculine scent intermingling with that of his soap and aftershave. The minty taste of toothpaste and the feel of his strong arms pulling me against his solid chest were overwhelming.

A swirl of emotion rolled through me as I let myself be swept away in that kiss, in the hard grip of his hands holding me against him. Lust, sure. But hope too. And a heartbreaking feeling of belonging. Finally belonging.

Mason broke the kiss and the spell too, and I collapsed back into the corner of the couch, my fingers touching my lips. For once, he looked affected too. Lips slightly swollen from our kiss, his hair was mussed, and his expression fiercely open.

"Now tell me that you didn't lie to me too," I said softly.

He rubbed his face with his hands, and when he looked back at me, a deep frown creased his mouth. "It would never work between us."

"Why not?" The question was too honest, left me open to too much hurt. But it fell from my lips before I could stop it. And it was a reasonable question, if too revealing. We were both cops. Both otherworlders—well, mostly. Sure, I wasn't a lycan, but I didn't think tradition alone would keep Mason Sanderson from anything he really wanted.

"Because I can't be with anyone," he said firmly.

"And I suppose the 'why' is a big damn secret." The man was turning me into a potty mouth but I didn't have the strength to care, and my mother's lessons had faded to the back of my mind. I was tired. Tired of Mason's issues. Tired of my own.

He didn't reply, but his face scrunched slightly, before returning to its expressionless norm. He turned away from me and leaned over, bracing his elbows on his thighs. And his gaze shifted to stare at his hands.

Suppressing a sigh of pure self-pity, I pushed up from the couch and went to bed.

Chapter Eight

A headache pounded from my neck. And with too many other aches and pains throbbing through my body, I found I could no longer sleep. The clock on the nightstand revealed that it was still early. I'd slept less than four hours.

But the injuries didn't keep me awake when I should have rolled over to go back to sleep. It wasn't even the vampire who'd violated the sanctity of my home. It was Mason.

The lycan embodied contradiction. He said things that made it seem like he really cared about me, and his actions supported that theory. But every time I felt like I was getting close to him, sneaking in under his barriers, he pushed me back.

I stepped off the bed and tested my ankle experimentally. The swelling had gone down. It ached, but was manageable. I tottered to the bathroom and dressed, then made my way down to the kitchen. The room was well-organized—almost obsessively so—and I found the coffee easily. With a pot brewing, I wandered around the rest of the downstairs. Mason should have case files here somewhere. Hopefully not in his bedroom.

I found the room he seemed to use for an office. A small den off of the main living area sported a computer and a small stack of files. I flipped the top one open and glanced at the contents. Bingo. Case files.

The first folder held summaries and comments, both from the Chicago PD and Mason's own notes. I had missed surprisingly little on the first scene, and what I'd learned from Mason in the meantime filled in any blanks I'd had there. The vampire had his throat cut, and with the relatively small amount of blood on scene, they suspected he'd been killed elsewhere.

I frowned. There had definitely been blood on the scene. If Mason was right and he'd been moved there, then he must have been fresh when they'd done it.

I grabbed the second folder and flipped it open. Autopsy and crime scene photos greeted me, and I was suddenly glad I hadn't eaten yet.

Crinkling my nose in disgust, I forced myself to look over the pictures carefully. Back and forth between the photos and the report, I lost track of time.

"Coffee?" a low voice asked from the doorway.

I started, and then peered over my shoulder at Mason. "Oh, I forgot about the coffee. Thanks."

He nodded and handed me a steaming cup.

"Do you have photos from the other cases Isaiah is suspected in?" I took a sip of the coffee and choked. I looked up into Mason's wide eyes.

"Are you okay?" he asked.

"How much sugar did you use?" I plucked a tissue from the box on the desk and wiped furiously at my chin.

"Sorry, I don't use sugar, so I guessed."

He'd guessed wrong. Probably a good four spoonfuls wrong, and I liked my coffee sweet. I rubbed my tongue against the roof of my mouth and tried to break through the sweet, thick barrier that coated it.

I glanced at him as he searched a desk drawer for the files. Nice to know he wasn't perfect. He produced a thick folder which he set in front of me on the desk. I reached to open it and he put one hand on the file.

"These are pretty bad," he warned.

"I can handle it." Granted, I hadn't been a cop for as long as most at the detective rank, and had pretty much been placed at that level right out of the academy because of my unique ability. But I *was* a cop, and I'd worked with Claude for two years. That Mason thought to warn me that crime photos might not be fun to look at was a little condescending.

I thumbed through the pictures for a while and Mason worked on the computer. They were bad in that they were bloody and there were quite a few of them, but at least the vampire hitman didn't seem to torture his victims. Not to the extent I'd seen in other cases. And none of the other victims had coin images burned into their bodies.

"Do you want something to eat?" Mason asked after we'd been at the desk for a while.

I blanched. Even though those pictures weren't the worst I'd ever seen, breakfast was the last thing on my mind. "Not yet, thanks. But don't wait on my account." I flipped the casino crime scene photos open and frowned at them. Something was different, off, about the casino pictures compared to the others attributed to Isaiah.

"So you think the body in Casino Merveilleux was taken there after death?" I asked.

"Yes. You'll see the blood pooling below the bodies at the other crime scenes. That was missing."

I stared at the image of Jake Stone. "So Isaiah kills them by slitting their throats and allowing the blood to go to waste—pooled at the victim's feet. A tough thing for a vamp to do, especially with another vampire's blood. Shows he's one tough mother. And if Isaiah killed Jake Stone, there would have been no reason for him to vary from that." I flipped back to one of the other victim's photos, a close up of the neck. "Why do you think he didn't just kill Stone on the ship?"

"It's a very public place. There's only a small window where that room is closed to the public, and an even smaller window when there aren't any cleaning people in there. He didn't want to get caught."

I rubbed my temple. "You've got vics killed here in places as public as a Magister's front lawn. An art exhibit that opened less than thirty minutes after a vic was killed right in the middle of it." I shook my head. "Isaiah isn't afraid of being caught. It's almost like he relishes playing chicken with authorities."

Mason walked around the desk and peered at the photos in my hand. "The blood pattern from the hands is the same. Or very nearly."

He was right. The art exhibit vic had been posed very similarly to the one in Casino Merveilleux, and the blood beneath their arms was of similar amounts.

"Jake Stone was still alive when he was pinned to that

wall," I muttered, an idea forming quickly in my mind. "But he was hung lower," I said as I reached a shot from farther out. "How tall do you think Isaiah is?"

"Six feet five inches."

"These older vics were hung so that he could still reach their necks, but high enough a shorter man couldn't—not without standing on something." I handed him a picture of Jake Stone. "He's hung a foot lower than the others."

Mason frowned. "They aren't all exact. He could have just hung Jake lower."

I ignored Mason, mind too full of an idea that had formed while I stared at the macabre photos. I flipped through the pictures until I found one of Jake's gaping neck wound. Swallowing hard, I focused on the injury.

"It's imperfect," Mason said, as if reading my mind. He grabbed several photos off the top of the stack on my lap and flipped to another neck wound, this one of a previous victim. The similarities to Jake's wounds were obvious. And the differences subtle.

But there *were* differences.

"Is it just me or does that look like one clean slice, whereas Stone's looks like he's been cut a couple of times over the same area? Dr. Martinson mentioned that it wasn't a clean slice, and it didn't look like one when we saw the body. But this…"

"You're right. The casino vic's wound is bigger. Again, like he was slashed more than once over a small area." He grimaced. "And not quite as deep."

I nodded. "Big enough maybe to cover a bite. Martinson said there were some marks in the wound that seemed inconsistent with the knife." The victim attributed to Isaiah had his neck sliced so cleanly and deeply that bits of his spine could be seen. "We should go through the other pics. Make sure none look like the casino victim's."

Mason tossed the pic back in the pile and then gripped my chair back. "How did I miss that?"

"You saw a neck wound matching that of a hired killer who happened to be in the city at the time — that's a big damn coincidence. If that's even what it was. Could be he's here just to throw you." I fingered the picture thoughtfully. "And the wounds are very similar. The setup is similar. Heck, they both even have a similar amount of blood on their clothes. I'll bet it was supposed to match Isaiah's handiwork exactly. But whoever killed Jake Stone didn't have Isaiah's self-control. Hell, he might have even been murdered where we found the body. He was just mostly drained of blood from a vampire bite before his neck was cut."

Mason cursed under his breath, and I didn't bother reassuring him again. Anything I could come up with wouldn't make him feel any less irritated with himself.

"Let's go eat," I said instead.

Despite the pictures, my stomach greeted Mason's omelets with enthusiasm. The man could cook. Over breakfast we chatted about neutral topics. Like if we thought my fellow detective, Mac, would actually go through with her recent engagement. I argued that she would without a doubt. Mason, who hadn't worked with Mac since shortly after she'd met her fiancé, argued that the woman just wasn't the type.

And we talked about the weather and football.

"What kind of fair weather fan are you?" I glared over the last bite of my omelet. "The Bears will go all the way this year, and anyone who doubts it isn't a real fan."

Mason laughed and the sound filled the air around me. The load on my shoulders lightened, and while I didn't want to rock the boat just yet by insisting on accompanying him to investigate today, I decided that he couldn't be all that mad at me if he was willing to laugh like that.

"I think we should go talk to Jake Stone's wife today," Mason said, and the amusement drained from his face, leaving behind a determined expression. "I think you were right. You should talk to her."

Hope blossomed in my chest, for more things than just getting to work the case with Mason, but I quickly pushed it down. I couldn't afford to think past this problem just yet. And just because Mason was willing to work with me didn't mean that he was interested in anything else.

I searched my mind for a clever retort, something that would say "thanks" without being too revealing. Finally, I settled for, "Sounds good."

He nodded. "Guess we should get going."

I almost sighed as the camaraderie we'd just bathed in faded, and only cool professionalism remained.

"Sure."

We bundled up quickly and headed for Mary Stone's house. Mason parked across the street and asked if I could feel anything in the house.

I closed my eyes and let my other sight settle over me. Mason, his aura sharp and powerful and so close, caught my attention first. I almost jumped. He'd faded like Claude already. I could sense him if I wanted to, but his aura no longer attracted my attention constantly. It had happened so subtly that I hadn't even noticed. Sure made concentrating around him easier.

I turned my attention to the victim's house. I could sense Mary Stone in there. She was on the near side. Had she already seen us? No other oh-dub energy caught my senses.

"Can't feel anyone from here. Other than the succubus," I said. I blinked and forced my focus back to Mason and the very solid world around us.

"Could someone be in there that you can't sense?"

"Sure. A human. Or a very weak oh-dub. But at this distance, it's not likely they'd evade my senses when I concentrate."

"All right, then. But you sense anything out of the ordinary, then you get the hell out." He pointed at the digital clock built into his dash. "Fifteen minutes, then I'm coming in."

I suppressed a sigh. Fifteen minutes wasn't long, but hopefully it would be enough time.

"See you in fifteen," I agreed.

I treaded carefully over the ice and snow until I reached Mary Stone's door, then I knocked briskly.

She didn't seem surprised to see me when she opened the door to admit me, and I guessed that she'd probably seen us outside her window. Dark circles ringed her eyes, stark against her too-pale face. Only two days had passed since I'd last seen her, yet she looked like she'd lost weight in that brief amount of time.

She got us coffee and we sat across from each other in her living room.

"How are you holding up?" I sipped the coffee and

examined her over the rim. This was more than just losing her husband. The woman looked positively haunted.

She hesitated, a pained expression on her face. "I've been better."

"I'm sorry for your loss," I said automatically. "And I'm sorry to bother you today. But you haven't been entirely honest with us, Mary."

The cup of coffee shook in her hands as she set it back on the table.

"Tell me about Nicolas."

She flinched as if I'd hit her. "How did you—"

"That's not important, is it?" I took a deep breath. "I know that this is hard for you. But you can trust me. And right now, I think you need someone in your corner."

Eyelashes fluttering to combat tears, she nodded. "I could use that right about now." Her voice was shaky and thin.

I moved to sit next to her on the couch and took her hand in mine. I gave it a quick squeeze before releasing her. "Tell me."

"It all started very innocently. Nicolas needed someone to decorate his new home." She looked down at her hands. "I'm an interior designer, you see."

Innocently? Fat chance. I was certain that the succubus sitting next to me probably believed what she said. But I had no doubts as to why Nicolas Chevalier had decided to hire her to decorate his home.

"Well, one thing led to another. I just…he's a very charming man."

Of course he was. The vampire was at least a couple hundred years old. Seducing his coworker's wives was no doubt a skill he'd cultivated during that time. "You had an affair."

"Yes," she whispered, gaze firmly affixed to her lap.

"And your husband found out?"

Her hands twisted, gripping each other for support. "He did."

"I'm guessing he objected pretty strongly."

A gasp that sounded half like a laugh escaped her. But there was no humor in her voice when she spoke. "Jake was livid. He threatened to complain to the Magister. Threatened to kill Nicolas."

Young Jake Stone loved his wife. But the relatively weak vampire would have had no chance against Nicolas. And would the Magister have acted? Against his own son? Perhaps. If only to tell Nicolas to stay away from Mary.

"What happened next?" I asked. Energy vibrated off of her, like she would explode if she didn't get this out. And I wanted to ask her the tough questions, but I had to ease into it. For all that she'd told me, she wasn't entirely comfortable yet.

She shrugged, and stared at her hands, looking so miserable that I almost reached out to her again. "Jake left. I guess he went to talk to the Magister, or to Nic. I'm not sure. When he came back, he was still angry. I'd never seen him like that before." She looked up and the pain in her eyes twisted my heart. She'd cheated on her husband with a very dangerous man, had probably gotten him killed, but I couldn't help but feel for her as the real weight of her decisions crashed onto her shoulders.

I gave her an encouraging half smile, but I didn't speak.

"I knew Jake was a vampire when we started seeing each other. It was part of the draw…just a little taste of danger, you know?"

I nodded like I knew, but I didn't really. Mason was the most dangerous man I'd ever had feelings for. Maybe he was dangerous. And in the right circumstances, I was certain he could be very dangerous indeed. But that didn't draw me. It was the very human man beneath the power, and the sense that a part of him ached for something he sensed in me. And part of me saw something it needed in him.

"But Jake…" She took a shuddering breath. "Jake was a good person. A simple man who just wanted a simple life. Why couldn't I give him that?" Her voice broke.

The very thing that had attracted Mary to her husband was the same thing Nicolas Chevalier had in spades. Danger. But the suggestion of danger in Jake hadn't prepared Mary to deal with the real thing.

"Did Nicolas kill your husband, Mary?" I asked gently, doing everything I could to keep the fear surging within me from my voice. This was big. Huge. Bigger than my ability to deal with it on my own. And it would even be tough with Mason at my side. Why the hell was Claude out of town this week of all weeks?

Mary jumped as if a jolt of electricity shocked her. "No! I mean, I don't know. You're asking me to—"

"I'm not asking you to do anything but tell me the truth, Mary."

The panic coming off her was palpable, and her eyes practically vibrated. "I don't know who killed him. I…" She glanced around the room as if only now discovering where she was. "I'm sorry, but you have to go."

"But—"

"Go!" she screeched.

Chapter Nine

"Something isn't right. She didn't tell me everything," I said for at least the fifth time since we'd arrived at Mason's house with our take-out Chinese food. Mary Stone had been impossible to reason with after she'd told me to go, and I was pretty certain that the woman had been prepared to physically toss me out despite my sidearm if I hadn't left when I did.

Mason threw up his hands, sending a small bit of rice flying onto the table. "Then we should go back. Press her for more information."

I sighed. "Let's give her the night. Go back in the morning. Maybe an extra night of thinking about her husband will loosen her tongue." I knew without a doubt that the likelihood of Mary Stone confiding anything more in me tonight was almost nonexistent. She was too emotional, too scared.

"You know it's possible that the affair and the murder aren't connected, right?"

My mouth dropped open. "She was cheating on one vamp with another, more powerful vampire, and he was killed by a vampire. And you think they aren't connected?"

"I said that didn't mean they were necessarily connected, not that they weren't for sure. I'm just saying, Nicolas Chevalier has an ironclad alibi."

I frowned. Much as I hated to admit it, Mason was right. "Too ironclad. Like he planned it that way," I muttered.

Mason shrugged and dumped a small pile of honey glazed walnut shrimp on his plate.

"Does Nicolas Chevalier strike you as the kind of man who would fight his own battles?" I asked.

"Nic Chevalier strikes me as the kind of snake who hides in the shadows unless there's a fight he's certain to win. Even then, I think he'd cheat, just to be sure."

My hand paused over my Mongolian beef. I hadn't expected quite such an honest assessment from Mason, but I guessed I shouldn't have been surprised. He wasn't the type to pull punches or bullshit to keep people happy. "You're right. And I think he's the type to hire out a hit on someone like Jake to make sure he had an ironclad alibi when we came calling."

"I suspect you're right."

I tapped my chopsticks together and watched Mason finish off the shrimp and a box of Kung Pao chicken. Man, lycans could eat. I laughed.

"You're like a teenage boy."

He flashed his teeth. "Am I?"

A shiver danced up my spine but I ignored it. "Yes. My brother used to eat like that." A flash of my brother's face, now vague since it had been so long since I'd seen him, touched my mind. "Of course, I think he still eats like that. But last I saw, he was developing quite the potbelly."

Mason's brows shot up to meet his hairline. "Are you accusing me of having a potbelly?" He leaned back and felt his stomach, as if worried he might find a new bulge.

I almost choked at the sight, and drank a gulp of soda to clear my throat.

"Don't let the sight of my awesome abs rob you of your breath, my dear."

I breathed in the soda I was trying to clear my throat with, and then coughed half of it into my napkin. Mason ran around the table and pounded my back, amusement and worry competing on his face.

"Stop it," I finally gasped out. "I give!" I waved the soda-covered napkin in the air. "You and your awesome abs win."

He chuckled and returned to his seat. When I didn't cough or gasp for a few minutes, he resumed his mission to eliminate the chance of leftovers, and I settled in to watch him.

"So you have a brother?"

I blinked. "Yes. An older brother and a younger sister." I kept my voice neutral, but something must have given me away.

"Not close?" His tone was as neutral as my own, but it didn't fool me.

"No." And I didn't want to talk about it.

Seeming to understand, Mason nodded. "Me either."

I wanted to drop the subject. My family was a sore spot for me—or if I was honest, a festering, bloody wound—but I couldn't help my curiosity about his.

"You have siblings?"

He grimaced. "Yes."

"Let me guess. All younger." There was no way an older brother or sister had ever pushed around the man in front of me.

"How'd you know?"

I picked up a chopstick and tapped it against my plate. Talking about family was a bad idea—like opening a door to a room you know contains a beast that will chew you up if you let it. "Are you close?"

"Used to be." He wiped his mouth with a napkin, leaving some food still on his plate. Apparently there was a subject that could rob the lycan of his voracious appetite.

"What happened?" It was wrong of me to press, but I couldn't seem to help myself.

He leaned back in his chair and crossed his arms as if deciding how best to answer me. Finally he said, "I screwed up. Someone got killed."

I opened my mouth to ask one of a million questions that statement pushed into my mind, but he waved his hand at me.

"That's enough about me for one night." His eyes narrowed. "Are you close to your family, Astrid?"

Something in his expression said that he already knew the answer to that question, but I replied anyway. "No."

"Why not?"

I took a deep breath and let it out in a *whoosh*. "Someone screwed up," I said finally. "But no one got killed."

He gave me a wry smile for my lame joke and I couldn't help but smile back.

We settled in to lighter conversation and cleared the table together. Charlie came in and watched from the doorway, looking as unimpressed as only a cat could. Mason shot him the occasional frown, but didn't try to shoo him out. A good thing, because I would have had to chill the mood by yelling at him. Despite the oddly comfortable repartee, my mind kept slipping back to think about Mason's family. Had his family abandoned him as completely as mine had me? What could he have done to cause a death?

I wiped my hands on a dishtowel and Mason's chest brushed my back as he reached around me to put a glass in the sink. I stiffened involuntarily, and he went still behind me, the material of his shirt softly touching mine. Heat emanated from him, and my mind spit out the fact that lycans burned hotter than humans by a few degrees.

"Astrid," he whispered, and his breath tickled my neck.

Mind wrestling with my body, I turned around. And his arms moved to press into the counter on either side of me, trapping me within them. The humor that had ridden his expression since dinner was gone, and intensity burned in his eyes again. His nostrils flared, as if scenting me.

I opened my mouth to say something—anything—to break the sudden sharp tension between us. But his mouth took mine before I could utter a single word.

I thought I'd gotten used to Mason's kisses, enough to know what to expect, anyway. But this was different. Despite the hard passion in his gaze, he took my mouth gently. Soft and smooth, his lips moved against mine. And then his tongue slipped in and I moaned quietly.

He enfolded me in his arms, still moving almost carefully. Wrapped up against him I suddenly felt warm—and safer than I'd felt since my world had imploded when I was a teenager.

I pulled back, fear crawling into me as I realized how comfortable I was getting in his arms.

"Wait." My tension leaked out into my voice and he stopped, eyes fluttering open, dark gray and so full of passion I almost told him to forget about waiting.

"I can't do this emotional rollercoaster, Mason," I said instead, and my body cried out in frustration. "Either you like me… Like this. Or you don't. Either you respect me and trust me — despite my lie to get onto this case — or you don't."

"Of course I like you." His eyes narrowed, wrinkling his skin and revealing a bit of his age. "And I don't think that one lie in that kind of situation makes you a bad person. I just —"

"What?" I asked.

"I lost someone, once. And because of that, I live like a damn hermit." He turned his eyes to the tile floor and stepped back, loosening his arms from around me. I almost sighed in frustration. "And that was okay. I deserved it. I wasn't worthy of having anyone else in my care — and didn't want to be responsible for another life."

"But dammit, Astrid. I'm tired of pretending that I don't care about you. That I haven't wanted you for years."

A solid lump grew in my throat, and I swallowed around it. I reached out and ran my fingertips down the side of his neck and down his shoulder. I wanted to tell him that I was half in love with him, and had been since that first kiss. "So do something about it," I said, instead.

Mason stopped moving, going as still as a statue in front of me. Then his eyes met mine, as hard and fervent as I'd ever seen them. My breath quickened, and I suddenly knew what a deer must feel like when it was stared down by a hungry wolf.

Then thinking disappeared, overrun by feeling. He was on me. Lips on mine, then sliding down my neck. He nipped at my collarbone and I clung to his shoulders. He plucked me up from the ground like I weighed nothing and carried me—toward the bedroom, I thought, but we only made it as far as the living room. As far as a plush rug made from a some sort of very soft animal fur that lay—quite stereotypically—in front of his fireplace.

I sank into the rug with Mason on top of me. His hands and mouth seemed to be everywhere, touching and tasting. I ran my hands over the muscles of his chest and shoulders, and through his soft hair. My mind whirred. Mason held me in his arms. Mason kissed me and wanted me. Mason cared about me.

I tugged at his shirt and he pulled it off, revealing a chiseled and perfect chest, not to mention the hard abs I'd teased him about earlier. Definitely no potbelly there. He tugged my scoop-neck shirt down until he reached my bra. Pushing my clothing down beneath my breast, he took a quick breath then pulled my nipple into his mouth. Sucking and nibbling and massaging, he made me cry out.

As if by magic, the rest of our clothes seemed to melt away under Mason's skillful hands. Hot chest moving against my sensitive breasts, he kissed me again. I felt myself writhing beneath him. I had to have him. Now.

I slid my hands down his hard back to grip his butt. Mason growled, and I moaned when I felt him press against my heat.

With one quick motion of his hips, we were joined. The air rushed out of me as he filled me to the brink, too hot against me and inside me to be a normal man. And around me, my other sense could feel his lycan energy crawling over me, filling my lungs with his scent, surrounding me. Uniting us. I cried out his name, and he called something that might have been mine.

He started moving, and the effort of going slowly so I could get used to the sensation was written all over his face.

But slow wasn't enough. I was so close. I gripped his ass hard and met his thrusts. I nipped at his shoulder.

"Fuck," he gasped. Then as if he could no longer contain himself, he moved, hard and fast. Deeper than before. And I cried out his name again as my vision was flooded with sparks and my body overcome by sensation. Mason called out, and I felt him jerk in my arms, pushing into me faster, harder, until I almost couldn't bear the sensation anymore. Then with a guttural moan, he stiffened above me, and then stilled.

Chapter Ten

Charlie stretched and rolled over to peer at me upside down from where he'd made a nest of Mason's pillow. I blinked at him dumbly for a few seconds as I got my bearings. Mason's house. Mason's room. Mason's bed.

I pushed up from the plush king-sized bed and glanced around the room, clutching the sheet to my chest. Decorated in large, masculine furniture, the room felt homey, if a bit bachelorish. It fell suddenly silent, and I realized that the shower had been running and filling the air with background noise. Before I could react to that, the bathroom door opened.

Mason stepped out and my breath caught. A man should not be allowed to look like that. Skin and hair damp from the shower, with a towel wrapped lazily around his waist, he looked like sin incarnate. And when his eyes met mine, I melted.

"Morning," he said, voice rough.

"Good morning." I couldn't help the heat rising up my neck to encompass my face, so I glanced down at my hands.

I sensed movement, and when I looked up, Mason stood less than a foot in front of me. He leaned down and gave me a soft kiss on the lips, and suddenly the awkwardness lifted. I touched his face softly. He stepped back and smiled at me, and I grinned.

His gaze shifted. "Is your cat on my pillow?"

I gave Charlie a sidelong glance. "He's just…making himself comfortable?"

Mason gave Charlie a disgusted glare. A look the cat returned with more haughtiness than the lycan could compete with. "Want some breakfast?"

Remembering the fabulous omelet he'd made before, I answered without thinking. "Absolutely."

He disappeared back into the bathroom and I trotted off to the spare bath where I'd already placed my essentials. A quick shower later, I dressed. Then I almost ran down the stairs when the smell hit me. Only my weak ankle and the tiny bit of self-control I was able to muster slowed my descent.

A small banquet greeted me. Eggs and coffee and bacon. Even pancakes. An embarrassing noise rumbled from my abdomen at the sight, and Mason grinned and handed me a plate.

"This isn't breakfast. It's a feast!"

He chuckled. "Well you took a while getting ready so I had some time to fill. It was either that or chase your cat."

I managed to not stick my tongue out at him. I'd gotten ready in record time. Not that I was high maintenance or anything, but I did have a hard time getting out of a nice, hot shower. Especially with my injuries from escaping the vampire at my townhouse, and the new, more pleasant aches I'd acquired with Mason the night before.

And what a night it had been. After our passionate coupling in front of his fireplace, we had retreated to his room. We'd spent most of the night alternatively making love and talking. We didn't touch on the subject that seemed to be a sensitive one for both of us—family—but we talked about everything else. From our shared love of Lou Malnati's pizza, to our shared obsession with old, cheesy horror flicks.

Mason handed me a cup of coffee and I glanced at it suspiciously. "I think we should go talk to the widow again today," I said.

Mason nodded. "Okay. But I'm coming in this time." He waved at the cup. "Try it. If you're not too scared, that is."

As if. But when I took a sip, I made sure to take only a small bit into my mouth. The blend of sugar and cream swirled around the bite of the coffee. Perfect. I gave him a small smile, but kept the conversation on business.

"Okay, but no flexing until I try a nicer approach first." Maybe he could convince her to be more helpful.

He puffed his chest out. "I don't flex, except when absolutely necessary."

"You keep the gun show under wraps, mister." I snickered and he gave me a quick preview of the show.

We finished our breakfast in good spirits and headed to Mary Stone's home. She opened the door after the third time I hit the doorbell and knocked. She wore a pissed off expression on her face.

"I don't know anything else," she said, hazel eyes flashing.

I shouldered past her with Mason at my back. She

allowed us through and shut the door behind us. She turned to face us with her hands on her hips, and a frown cutting into her lovely face.

"It's obvious there's something you're holding back. Something important. Maybe something that implicates Nicolas Chevalier."

She glared at me, so I continued. "We will protect you, but we need to know everything that you do."

"I told you—"

"If you don't want to do it for your husband, then do it for the next one. The next widow. Save her from your fate."

Her expression faltered, then hardened again. "I don't care about some other widow. You need to get out of my house."

I opened my mouth but Mason beat me to the punch. "Vampires like that don't leave loose ends, sweetheart. You don't cooperate with us then you're as good as dead. It might not happen this week, or even this month. But it will happen. And you'll be as dead as the husband you just buried."

"I'll be just fine as long as I don't say anything to you people!"

"Is that what they told you?" Mason stepped closer to her, moving into her space. She took a step back, real fear crossing her features. "Because they lied. Let me guess. A phone call? A few hushed sentences telling you to keep your mouth shut? They won't let you live, Mary. They'll fucking kill you, and you know that."

She seemed to struggle to breathe for a brief moment. Then her face crumpled into utter misery, and tears leaked down her tense cheeks. Mason had been right about the phone calls. I made a mental note to check up on that, but we were dealing with professionals. The phones would be throwaways, untraceable. And it was hardly likely that Nicolas Chevalier had made the calls himself.

"God, you're right," she cried. "I'm so fucking dead."

"Not if you tell us the truth," I said, voice as gentle as I could manage under the circumstances. Her husband was probably dead because she'd had an affair, and the only thing that prompted her to cooperate at all was the threat against her own life. I wanted to kick her, but instead I grasped her shoulder. A quick show of support before she turned and grabbed a hold of Mason, crying and blubbering into his chest.

I ground my teeth together as Mason did his best to calm her down. An unexpected spike of jealousy ran through me at the sight of the curvy succubus tucked against him. He peered at me from over her head, a look of panic on his face, and the jealousy dissipated.

Once the succubus had calmed enough to speak, Mason sat her on the couch. She took the glass of water I offered with a nod of thanks and drank half of it in one long gulp.

"Tell us what happened," Mason said. His voice was soft, but the order was unmistakable.

"A woman came and took Jake that night. He didn't leave on his own, like I said."

"Did you catch her name? What did she look like?" I asked.

"I don't know her name. She was Asian. Pretty. She doesn't look like much, but I'd seen her before, hanging around Nicolas. He doesn't spend time with weak vampires unless they have something he wants, so I knew she was probably pretty strong. Or…one of his girls. But she didn't seem the type, you know? All dressed in leather and never smiling."

Something he wanted. Like hanging around Jake to get close to his wife? I took some notes down and watched Mary Stone expectantly. The woman she described had to be the one we'd seen with Nicolas and the Magister at the casino. How many leather-clad Asian women could Nicolas hang around with on a regular basis?

"And there's something else…"

"What is it?" Mason asked.

"Jake mentioned…well I don't think he was going to the Magister just to complain about me. He said that he knew stuff about Nicolas. That he'd worked with Nicolas doing things that the Magister would like to know about. I think he was going to go to the Magister with some real information. Something that could have gotten Nic in serious trouble."

"Did your husband work with Nicolas? I mean, other than at the law firm?" I asked.

She flinched. "He would help him out. Evenings and weekends. Do errands for him. I think at first it was so Nic could get me alone. But after a while he started to trust Jake enough to have him work on things he didn't want anyone to know about. Jake started getting secretive about what he was doing for Nicolas."

"But you don't know what he did for him?" I pressed.

She shook her head.

"Tell us more about the woman who took Jake." Mason's jaw twitched. He didn't like this one bit, and neither did I.

"Jake seemed nervous around her too, but he couldn't talk to me without her hearing. She had him go out first, and when she was leaving…" The succubus swallowed hard, and then took a sip of water.

"Yes?" I tried to keep my impatience out of my voice, but we finally had a lead and I was eager to get out of this house and follow it.

"As she was leaving, she turned and said, 'Nicolas sends his regards.'" She shivered and ran her hands up and down her arms.

"But you didn't actually see Nicolas? Did he say anything to you at the funeral? Or anything since?" Mason asked.

She shook her head, and her voice was dull when she spoke. "No. He's been treating me like a stranger. Offering his arm, condolences. Acting the perfect Magister's son."

"Anything else you can tell us about the woman who was here?"

She thought about that for a few tense seconds. "Like I said, she was dressed like some kind of biker. And she had this old coin that she played with while she talked. Like constantly."

Blood rushed through my ears, so loudly I almost missed her next words.

"I half expected her to pull it out from behind my ear like some sort of cheesy magician."

Chapter Eleven

"We need to get out of here." I fidgeted next to Mason and blew out a gust of breath that condensed in the chill air surrounding us as we stood on the sidewalk in front of Mary Stone's house.

He glanced up from his cell. "It'll be a while before I can get agents out here to take care of her."

"Call Vasquez. This is a joint investigation. He can get a black and white here in five."

Mason frowned but made the call. Seven minutes later, a patrol car pulled up and we were free to go. Mason, normally a conscientious driver, peeled out of the widow's neighborhood and broke every speed law possible on our way to the Magister's house.

Except house was too common a word for Luc Chevalier's abode. Something like manor or estate fit it better. I'd been here before, but always with Claude. And without him, it somehow felt more oppressive than normal, even with Mason's solid presence beside me. Maybe because this world—the vampire's—was even more foreign to him than it was to me.

We strode to the front door and Mason hit the doorbell, then knocked loudly for good measure. I pulled my coat tighter against my body.

A stiff, balding man in a creased suit answered the door. I recognized him from the other times I'd visited. What had he seen during his years of service to the Chevalier family? I couldn't even begin to imagine.

I stepped in front of Mason before he could yell at the butler and demand to see Nicolas and Luc immediately— thus guaranteeing us a long wait.

"Hello. We're sorry for the intrusion, but we need to speak with the Magister at his earliest convenience. Could you tell him that we're here? It's very important." I gave him a tight smile and his nose dropped slightly from its perch high in the air.

"Detective Holmes. If you and your guest will follow me."

I started at my name. The man must have a great grasp of names to recognize me, especially without Claude at my side. But such a thing would be part of his job. And to work for the Magister, the man would have to be very good at his job.

Instead of leading us to the small office right off the entryway where Luc Chevalier generally met professional guests, the butler led us to an opulent living room. The room was equipped with two large couches and a loveseat along with a couple of oversized puffy chairs, all situated around a coffee table. Rich leather coated most of the furniture. It blended nicely with the dark hardwood floors and intricately woven rugs. Two other chairs sat facing a fireplace, which was in full burn, fire licking at logs piled high. No gas fireplace for the Magister.

The butler disappeared and Mason pushed his hands into his pockets and leaned against a couch instead of sitting. To the casual observer, he might appear relaxed. But I could see the predatory wariness of his gaze, the barely tensed muscles of his body that were ready to spring into action at a moment's notice.

And I remembered exactly how that fighter's body felt under my hands, under my lips. How it felt poised over mine. How my body responded to his.

Our eyes met, and something of my thoughts must have leaked out in my expression, because the tension in his body increased and he looked at me with his hunter's gaze. My mouth went dry, and I licked my lips. He took a step toward me. My body buzzed in anticipation.

"Agent, Detective," the Magister's voice entered the room at the same time he did. "What brings you to my home, today?"

Mason swerved, and instead of pouncing on me, he reached out and shook the Magister's hand.

I blinked. I'd felt the thrum of power that said the Magister was home when we had pulled up, but I hadn't noticed his proximity before he entered the room. I shook myself. Mason Sanderson was dangerously attractive if he could distract me—even for an instant—from the approach of a vampire of Luc's caliber.

"We're here to ask for your assistance in finding one of your people. A person of interest in a case. And to inform you of our interest in questioning her." We didn't have to inform him, strictly speaking, but I was glad Mason had included that little line. I'd insisted during the drive over, but I hadn't been entirely certain he would actually say it.

Luc's expression didn't change. "I will endeavor to help the police however I can. Who are you looking for, and what is your interest?"

"We're looking for Min, the woman we met when we spoke with you earlier this week. And she is a person of interest in a murder."

If a pin had dropped somewhere in the room for three seconds after Mason's statement, I imagined that it was almost quiet enough that I would have heard it. Ridiculous, of course. The dull roar of the fire alone would have overshadowed such a small sound, but the Magister went quiet and still in such a way that only vampires were capable of. In a way, I imagined, that was only possible for dead things.

The beats passed and Luc lit back up with life and polite concern. "Is this related to Jake Stone's death?"

"Yes," Mason said simply. We needed the Magister's help to find Min—we didn't even know her last name, if she had one, and time was of the essence. And Mason wasn't going to offer any information that he didn't strictly have to. But we did need the Magister. There was a small chance that Min wasn't the one who picked up Jake—but I doubted it, given her close relationship with Nicolas. But if Mary Stone said it wasn't her, we'd need the Magister's help to track down the woman who picked up Jake the night he died.

"Gerald?" Luc called. He didn't raise his voice, but it carried.

The butler—Gerald—reappeared from the way we'd

come in. "Sir?"

"Get me Nicolas's schedule, please."

Gerald gave the Magister a small bow and disappeared again.

"Why do you believe that Min, of all people, is responsible for this death?"

"That's need to know information," Mason said, voice tight.

The Magister stiffened. "Well, I need to know. That is, if you want my help."

Mason looked like he was on the edge of saying something on the wrong side of the politeness scale, so I cut in before he could speak. "I'm sorry, Magister, but that's not something we can divulge. Surely you understand. Once the suspect is in custody, we'll be able to share more." I wasn't at all certain of that, but the Magister relaxed a hair at my words.

"Sir. Master Nicolas's schedule for the week." The butler moved so quietly, I hadn't even noticed him reentering the room. But he carried computer printouts. I caught a glimpse as he handed it to the Magister.

Lo and behold, even old vampires used Outlook.

"Fucking vampires," Mason growled.

I glanced up from where I was looking through a stack of files at Mason's kitchen table.

"Didn't go well with Nicolas?"

"Arrogant bastard." He dropped his keys onto the table and yanked at his jacket.

"Let me guess. He had no idea Min could have been involved in something so terrible, and he has no idea where she might be found?"

"Pretty much."

After Mason and I found Nicolas, a patrol car took me back to Mason's house and Mason questioned Nicolas alone. I'd decided not to argue with the lycan. He'd seemed edgy, and was right when he said that a cop currently on administrative leave questioning a Chevalier at OWEA headquarters was a bad idea. I'd considered pointing out that I'd been with him in the field questioning witnesses, but I didn't want to push my luck. Besides, I got the feeling that Mason mostly just didn't want me breathing the same air as Nicolas Chevalier.

"Did you release him?"

"We'll have to by morning. But I'll put a unit on him. If he moves wrong, we'll know it." He picked up one of the papers I was looking through. "What are you working on?"

"Just trying to connect some dots." I rolled my shoulders and tried to work out some of the tension. "That coin is bothering the hell out of me."

Mason moved behind me and then his hands were on my shoulders. Massaging gently, he worked on my knots. I let out a noise that was far too close to one of Charlie's purrs. "Oh... You can stop that, never."

Mason chuckled, a low sound that vibrated from his chest. "So what about the coin is bothering you?"

I closed my eyes and tried to concentrate. It was so tempting to just melt into a puddle. "How it got out of evidence."

"With money like the Chevalier's, he could have had

it spelled out of there. Hell, he could have paid a cop off. Or just a good thief. Evidence lockers are pretty secure, but someone really good could still manage. With the help of a little magic."

I grimaced. He was right. We'd probably never know for sure unless we got Min and gained a full confession. But I didn't have to like it.

"Are you hungry?" Mason asked, and his hands gave my shoulders one last squeeze before he headed to the kitchen.

I followed him and watched, mesmerized, as he whipped up a small feast. My offers to help were waved off, so I enjoyed the show.

"Where'd you learn to cook so well?" I asked, then took another bite of the most well-cooked steak I'd had since I could remember.

"My mom," he said gruffly.

Keep things light. "I wish mine had passed on such a useful skill."

His eyebrows rose. "Your mom didn't cook?"

I snorted. The idea of my mother in the kitchen was too funny. "No. She ordered things from the cook. She never would have deigned to get her hands dirty."

"Is she—I mean you talk about her in the past tense."

The bite of steak I'd consumed suddenly formed a rock in my stomach. "No, she's not dead or anything. She's just no longer in my life. Or, I guess it's more accurate to say that I'm no longer in hers."

Mason just waited silently, eating his asparagus and eyeing me over his fork. Leaving it up to me if I wanted to continue.

"My mother is married to one of the Leighs. I changed

my last name. Took her maiden name when I graduated high school."

Mason chewed his food slowly, before swallowing it and taking a sip of wine. Thinking about the only Leighs worth mentioning as if the name would mean something all on its own, no doubt.

"Any relationship to Natalie Leigh and her family?" he asked. Natalie Leigh was the department's witch, or near enough. An independent contractor who the local police departments consulted when they needed the service of a Covenant witch.

"She's a cousin." I shook my head. Telling him half the story wasn't enough, and wasn't fair. I'd opened the door. Time to walk through. "The man I thought was my father until I was a teenager is Atticus Leigh."

Mason whistled low under his breath, and I could hardly blame him. I'd just uttered the name of one of the most powerful Covenant witches in the country and included the word "father" in the same sentence.

I took a long drink from my wine glass. "At first, they just thought I was an unfortunate screw up of nature. It happens sometimes, you know. A child born of a powerful witch couple has no magical ability. It's rare—but it does happen. Such children are usually ignored, but not exiled."

"But you're also a sensitive," Mason said thoughtfully.

"Yes. When I got old enough to start showing my very human power, my mom could no longer deny that she'd had a…dalliance. With a human. So my father had me shipped off to boarding school for the rest of my childhood, and now they pretend I don't exist."

Mason's grip around his wine glass tightened.

"It's not so bad. I have a small trust fund that ensures I'll never starve, even if I didn't have my income from the Force." My forced smile faltered. "I'm just never invited home."

"Fucking-a. How can your mom let him do that?"

A nervous laugh escaped me. "I'm pretty certain that most of my exile is due to her. Not that Atticus Leigh wants proof of his wife's affair hanging around, but I think her shame exceeds his."

Mason looked like he wanted to kill someone, so I tried to reassure him. "I'm fine, really. I'm not complaining. I got the best education money could buy, and was never abused—not really. Besides, I'm not the only person ever ostracized and banished from family gatherings, right?"

He grimaced. "About that…" He poured us both a new glass of wine.

More wine needed? This was bound to be interesting. I took a sip and waited.

"My family didn't really exile me. Not in the way yours did."

I frowned. "I thought you said someone died—that you no longer spoke with your family."

"I don't. But they didn't exile me. I guess you could say that I banished myself."

I set my wine glass down carefully. "So you're saying that you have a family out there just waiting to let you back into their lives—waiting to love you—and you *choose* not to talk to them?"

His eyes clouded over with regret. "I made a huge mistake, Astrid. And even if they weren't willing to punish me, someone had to. I haven't seen them since, nor have I changed forms."

"What did you do that was so awful? Who died?" How long had it been since he'd talked to them, since he'd changed?

"A girl I was supposed to marry."

My mouth went dry and I stared at him.

"It was arranged, clans of lycans still do that sometimes to strengthen the bonds. We were both willing." He shrugged and looked down at his half-finished meal. "I was ten years younger, in my early twenties. And she was beautiful."

My stomach swirled and wrenched. "And what happened?"

"She had a boyfriend before agreeing to the match. He followed her into the city. He didn't want to let her go. So the night before our wedding, he killed her, and then himself."

My mind raced. Did Mason love her? Is that why he'd never wanted to pursue me past that kiss until we were forced together because of this case? And God, how could he blame himself when someone else had killed her?

"I don't get how that's your fault," I said finally.

"She was under my protection. I should have stopped him. Should have saved her." Self-loathing and guilt cut across his features, transforming his normally hard, expressionless face into something raw and bloody.

"Mason. Her death wasn't your fault. And I think your family would agree with me, if you'd let them." Not only had he not talked to his family in a decade, he hadn't changed into his lycan form. It was a double punishment. He didn't get to be around the people who loved him, and he had robbed himself of the power he could gain by changing. And while he might someday talk to his family again, the power of his lycan form might never be regained. Changing wasn't easy for lycans. The process was difficult, and it only got harder if they didn't shift often. And by denying that change for years, Mason may have denied himself his natural birthright forever.

The mask dropped back over his face. "I can't do that. Not yet. I can't face them."

My heart twisted, and I battled the urge to hit him for being an idiot, or pull him into my arms and give him the comfort he so desperately needed. But I didn't think he'd thank me for either gesture, so I settled for pushing up from the table and carrying my dishes to the sink.

I was rinsing my glass after finishing the last couple of swallows of wine when I felt his heat behind me. He didn't touch me, just moved close enough that I could feel him.

"I swore that I'd never put myself in that position again. That I'd never consider a future with someone. Never care about someone like that again." His voice was soft, and I could feel his breath slide against my hair as he spoke.

"Did you love her?" I whispered, then bit my lip. I hadn't meant to ask that question, and I wasn't entirely sure I wanted to know the answer.

"I thought I did, at the time. And maybe I did, as much as I could, given our age and our short time together." His hand moved to my shoulder, touching me softly. He traced his fingertips down my arm. "But I don't think I really knew what being in love was...until I met you."

I tried to find my voice but couldn't. I wasn't able to force my body to turn around to face him either. Instead, I stood at the sink and shuddered as he slid my hair aside and kissed my neck.

I didn't move as his hands glided up to caress my back

and shoulders, down to my waist and around to my stomach. But my mind whirred. Here was a man—a wonderful, exciting, sexy man—who wanted me. Maybe even loved me. But his choice to cut himself off from the only thing I'd ever yearned for hurt me on a deep, foundational level.

But with his skillful hands touching me, his wet mouth against my skin, I could forget. For a little while.

I turned from the sink and he took my mouth with his, his arms slipping around me to pull me close. Desperation laced his kiss, and the fever of it touched me as well. His mouth opened and I tasted the wine on his tongue.

Holding me close, he kissed me until I burned for him. Our bodies melded together in a comforting embrace. Then he stepped back and took my hand.

We reached his bedroom and I stood at the end of the bed while he undressed me languidly. As each piece of clothing dropped, he would pause and kiss the skin it revealed. Passion laced his gaze, but something else too. Something tender and fragile.

I ran my hands through his hair and over his shoulders, kissing him when he drew near. But I didn't rush him. My body shook and I trembled when he finally lifted me onto the bed.

Mason undressed quickly and joined me. He covered my body with his and cradled me in his arms. Comfort and such a feeling of safety hit me that a rush of fear immediately followed it. There were too many what-ifs between us. Too many unresolved issues. Too many unanswered questions.

Mason moved from my lips to kiss my neck and worked his way down to my breasts. Taking my nipple into his mouth, he sucked and nipped until all coherent thought was forced out of my head.

He kissed his way down my stomach. Lower. His tongue touched my aching heat and I cried out and gripped his hair hard enough that he growled. But he didn't slow his assault. And within moments I was moaning and writhing against him. Calling his name and forgetting my own.

He slid back over me and kissed and bit my neck softly, then I could feel his hardness, nestled so close to where I desperately needed it.

"I love you," he murmured in my ear. But before I could process the words, he took me.

Thrusting hard within me, Mason lost the control he'd shown with his gentle assault all night. I held onto him, moving beneath his hard, sweat-soaked body to meet his every thrust. I cried out again when my body exploded beneath him, and his cry joined mine as he pushed himself into me as far as he could, and shuddered on top of me.

Realization hit as he held me in his arms, his words reverberating in my skull. I loved him too.

But could I trust him?

He'd turned his back on his family—his pack. And he'd been hot and cold with me. Kissing me one minute, and pushing me away the next. He was able to go on without the people he loved, the people he'd sworn to protect. If I loved him and he pushed me away, he'd move on. But I'd be broken.

How could I put my faith in someone who could so easily turn from those he loved?

Chapter Twelve

The sun didn't get a chance to rise before my eyes flew open the next morning. I wanted to stay in the heat of Mason's arms, but there was an itching in my muscles, just under my skin, that refused to let me relax. We had to get up. Get out there and look for Min. And I had to get away from Mason's embrace, where everything felt too comfortable, too safe. I had to think.

His arms tightened around me briefly before letting me go. Mason's eyes met mine and I gave him a small smile before grabbing the shirt he'd worn the night before from the corner of the bed. I threw it on and headed for the spare bathroom.

After a quick shower I felt almost normal. Almost like myself again. But his words still bounced around my mind, fighting for first position in my thoughts along with wondering how we were going to find Min, and how the hell they'd gotten that coin out of the evidence warehouse.

Mason was eating cereal when I reached the kitchen.

"Cocoa Puffs or Frosted Flakes?" he asked, face entirely too straight for a man who just offered me children's cereal. I grinned and he raised his nose up. "They're both very good, I'll have you know."

I laughed and grabbed the Frosted Flakes. Less than five minutes later, we were headed out.

Mason opened the door and waved for me to go first. I'd been wrong. His gallantry hadn't grown old. But the sight that greeted me on the other side of the door made my grin falter.

A white box with a large blue bow wrapped around it. The fancy kind of bow that has to be tied by hand, not stuck on. And the bottom of the box was rimmed with a dark liquid.

Mason already stared at the box, his posture stiff. His nostrils flared. Of course. He'd probably smelled it the second he opened the door.

"Blood?" I asked, already knowing the answer.

"Yes."

What the fuck is that? How the hell did they get it on your doorstep with an officer parked across the street? I wanted to fling the questions at him, but instead I asked, "Smell any explosives? Traps?"

"No. What do you see?" he asked, and I knew that he wasn't talking about my normal sight.

I closed my eyes and tried to calm down. The box didn't look hexed or trapped magically—no witchcraft traces were on it that I could sense. One distinctive energy clung to it heavily, seeping in and around the box. Another otherworlder power was there too, slighter, fainter, but fading more slowly than the other. Burnt coffee filled my nose even as a hint of strawberries touched my tongue

"Fucking vampires," I spat out. "And Mason…"

"What is it?"

I swallowed hard. "I think it's Mary Stone."

Mason's face was hard as granite when the police showed up. First OWEA units and techs, then—hot as a raging bull and just as fun to talk to—Lieutenant Vasquez.

The OWEA crime scene techs took their pictures and samples from the outside of the box before okaying Mason to open it. I watched as he swiftly cut the ribbon in three places to free the lid, and even though I was certain of what he would find, I couldn't look away.

A quick flip of his pocketknife under the cardboard and the still-open eyes of Mary Stone stared out at us. Accusation laced her expression. Blame. *You said you would keep me safe. You promised. I risked my life to help you and now my head is stuffed in a box.*

I swallowed bile and took an involuntary step back. But I still couldn't look away. This was my fault. I'd pressed her. Insisted that we make her tell us the truth. Promised to protect her.

Mason was talking. Giving out orders in his low but dangerous tone. Vasquez cursed into his cell phone. I closed my eyes and took a deep breath. I had to focus. I had to find the bitch that did this.

Nicolas had the perfect alibi, of course. He was at the police station all night. Going over what he knew of Min.

Handing over every location he knew she haunted. Except for the one where she currently hid—of that I had no doubt. He'd volunteered to stay and hand the information to the OWEA. Ever helpful. Ever the good citizen. Ever securing the best damn alibi possible.

A hand squeezed my arm and I opened my eyes. Mason looked concerned, but under that was something else. Something deadly.

"I'm taking a team. Min has been spotted at one of her haunts. Some vamp's house. You stay here with Vasquez and the others."

I opened my mouth to argue and he squeezed my shoulder, not hard, just enough to give me pause.

"I can't take you." He stepped closer. "It'd be totally against regulation. And—"

"And what?" I snapped. The whole thing put me on edge. Mary Stone was my witness, dammit. No way would she have given that info if I hadn't sensed she was holding back. If I hadn't forced her to tell.

"If something happened to you—"

"Mason—"

"No." His eyes flashed. "Not negotiable. Vasquez wouldn't let you go even if I asked."

I wanted to point out that he had never "asked" Vasquez anything. And that it was a damn poor excuse to leave me behind because he was scared I'd get hurt. But I wasn't an idiot. A vampire would run rings around me. I knew it. Mason knew it. But I'd worked the investigation too. I deserved to be in on the takedown. And I wasn't useless. My sensitive abilities could help them. Could make sure they weren't walking in to a trap.

But I wasn't going to win this argument, so I saved my breath. "Be careful," I said instead.

He nodded and gave me a small smile, a quick flash reserved just for me, then he was gone.

I examined the head until the coroner's office relieved us of it, then I stared blankly at case files, keeping my phone in hand in case Mason called. When Jarvis showed up, Vasquez exploded.

I hadn't thought to ask who'd been with the widow and how the hell they'd gotten to her with police protection. She should have been in a safe house. I wanted to smack myself for not asking sooner, but I'd been distracted. A dismembered head would do that. Getting left behind on a takedown would do that. Worrying about a man you might be in love with going up against a vampire would do that.

But when Jarvis arrived, the information came out pretty clearly.

Vasquez yelled until a vein on his forehead looked like it might burst from the pressure. Jarvis's body jerked at each of Vasquez's insults and curses, twitchy and imp-like. Like a lot of oh-dubs, his traits came out even more obviously when he was under pressure. And he did the only thing he could. Apologize profusely and try to explain what happened.

"I don't know if it was a spell or what," the imp said, voice drenched in desperation, and his hands wringing. "I didn't just fall asleep and not wake up while someone took her."

I almost blurted out the question that had been on my mind since Jarvis entered the room. Wasn't he supposed to be on administrative leave, too? Instead, I gave Vasquez a meaningful stare. He took me aside after reaming Jarvis.

"No evidence was found that he'd been involved, so he came back on duty yesterday," Vasquez said, voice pitched low to keep us from being overheard.

"Oh, yeah? Then why wasn't I brought back on?" I feared his response, but I had to know.

"You have easier access to the kind of spell that knocked everyone in that room out, so you're taking a little longer to clear." He waved at me to keep me from interrupting. "That you've been personally targeted isn't making this move any faster. But it is moving. I know they won't find any evidence against you, but shit moves slowly down at IA. Give it a couple more days."

I swallowed down the anger that pulsed in my throat, and forced a nod. A screaming match with Vasquez would get me exactly squat right now, and I had to stay focused.

So I turned away from my boss and looked at Jarvis. I felt a little sorry for him, but just a little. The memory of Mary Stone's sightless eyes kept me from real pity. But his words got me thinking, so I closed my eyes and looked at him—really looked. His imp energy coated him of course, and the vampiric energy I'd sensed on him at the casino crime scene touched him, too. Why did he stink of vampire?

Maybe I'd been wrong at the Casino Merveilleux. Maybe he hadn't gotten too close to the body. Maybe he was dating a vampire or something. My heart rate kicked up a notch at the thought, and I watched him carefully. The shadow of vampire energy muted the already subdued strobe light that signaled his imp heritage.

No sign of a spell or any witch magic. I pursed my lips. That didn't necessarily mean that he hadn't been spelled. A standard sleep spell would probably leave a bit of witch-tinged aura on him for a week after it was cast. But there were less run-of-the-mill spells that wouldn't linger. One or two that an amateur might even be able to cast. Though the actual casting would be illegal as hell for a non-Covenant witch.

Long minutes passed without word and I spent most of it going in and out of an almost meditative state, trying to focus on anything except for how long Mason had been gone, and how Vasquez's mood grew darker by the minute.

I kept finding my attention settling back on Jarvis's aura. He could just have a vampire girlfriend. If he did, that didn't automatically make him a suspect, but something wasn't adding up. There were too many coincidences. Too many things he seemed involved in—at least peripherally. The tinge of vampire aura all over him. The fact that the coin disappeared with him in the room. What if he hadn't really been knocked out by the blast, but had used the distraction to hide the coin, or pass it off to an accomplice?

Could he have accomplished that? I wasn't certain he'd been searched, but it was a possibility he'd have to have planned for. Maybe he'd stashed it? A trashcan or under another box? Hell, he could have counted on his reputation to keep him from being searched fully and just shoved it in his briefs. Risky, but possible.

I blinked at sudden movement in front of me. Jarvis was talking to Vasquez in low tones.

The coin. The fact that he had been watching Mary Stone—or should have been—before she was killed. And he stunk of vampire.

I needed more information. Not just on sleep spells. Mason had mentioned that the spell that knocked us all out at the evidence locker had likely been triggered from inside the warehouse. I'd dismissed it, knowing that was hardly a certainty. But how likely was it? My education as a witch had stopped while I was young and still learning histories, not actual spells.

I needed to reach out to someone who would know.

My dislike of speaking with Covenant witches extended far beyond just my immediate family. And I'd managed to avoid all but the slightest contact with my cousin, Natalie Leigh, who contracted as the department's Covenant witch on cases that required such services.

I slipped out to Mason's backyard with the excuse that I needed a breath of fresh air. No one shot me so much as a second glance. A quick call to information and my cell phone was ringing through to Natalie Leigh's office.

I'd expected her voicemail, or a secretary. Something to give me a little more time to steel my nerves. So when Natalie answered, I almost dropped my cell phone.

"This is Natalie Leigh," she said, voice bright like a customer service agent before you told them you wanted to disconnect your cable.

I cleared my throat. "Natalie. This is Astrid—Detective Astrid Holmes." Even to my own ears, my voice sounded a little breathless. "With the Chicago Paranormal Unit," I added lamely.

"Astrid. Yes, of course." Her voice maintained its professional tenor, but her words were hesitant.

"I'm calling to get your professional opinion," I said, as if we hadn't played together as children. Of all my family, I'd been closest to Natalie. She was an only child, and my brother was older and disinterested in his annoying little sister. Our mothers were sisters, so we had spent many hours together before either of us was old enough to even really know the difference between witches and humans, let alone how that big gap would tear us apart.

"Of course. Ask away."

I glanced over my shoulder at Mason's house to ensure I was still alone, then briefly described the spell that had knocked out Jarvis, Donaldson, and me the night the coin had been taken.

"So the spell took the power out and knocked you out simultaneously?"

"Yes. What I really need to know is how difficult that would be to cast from outside the room. Especially if a witch wasn't actually present."

"So you're talking spells attached to an object?"

"Exactly. No witch was close enough for me to sense." I was almost certain that an actual witch hadn't been present. Even with my concentration focused on the coin, I would have definitely sensed a witch close enough to cast that sort of spell on me.

Silence took over the line for a few seconds. Painful moments that I almost ached to fill with questions. Questions that had absolutely nothing to do with my case.

"If you couldn't sense them, then you're probably right about the object. For the spells to trigger together like that, they'd have to be woven together. Otherwise, one would have been cast before the other."

"So either the security feed would have seen us fall, or we would have seen the power fail before the knock-out spell hit us, if they weren't weaved into a single spell," I said, not really asking for clarification, but she gave it anyway.

"Yes, exactly. And Astrid, that's not an easy thing to weave together."

I glanced back at the house. "Are we talking Covenant?"

"Not necessarily. But this would be expensive, regardless of the provider. And it would have to be triggered in the actual room. The person who triggered it would have been immune as the caster."

"Leaving him to run around and do whatever he needed to do for the few minutes before anyone arrived to check on the alarm," I replied, excited now. But as the excitement hit, dread circled it. That meant exactly what I'd feared. Someone inside had triggered the spell. Someone like Jarvis.

"Alarm?" Natalie asked.

"Oh, yes. Whenever the power goes out in a restricted place like the evidence locker, it trips an alarm for a black and white to come check on the building. That's how they found us passed out." I frowned. "I guess that if he triggered the spell, then took the coin, he'd just have to pretend to be unconscious when the cops arrived to check."

"He? What coin?" Natalie paused. "He also could have had a second charm, to knock himself out after it was done. That would be an easier one to make and a cheaper one to get."

That idea was interesting. And quite possibly correct. "I can't really fill you in on all the details, right now. But a coin disappeared on a case I'm working from evidence. I think—I think it was enchanted."

Silence greeted my statement.

"We found burns, on the victim's body. They were burned in by the coin and they felt like witch to me—not exactly, but similar enough." I knew what I was saying wouldn't make much sense to Natalie, but she worked with the police enough to pick up enough to follow me, and while I had her on the phone, I might as well ask after the coin itself. "I'm pretty sure that the coin was more than a decoration."

"Was it old?"

"The coin? Yes. I don't know how old, but it looked pretty ancient. And the vamp energy on it suggested someone had owned it for decades—maybe centuries."

The sound of Natalie muttering to herself and pages flipping was her only response for a few seconds. "I'll have to do some research."

"Sounds good," I said.

"And, Astrid—"

"Yes?"

"It's nice to hear from you."

With those words reverberating through my mind, the line clicked dead. I stared at my phone for a few precious seconds, before heading back to the house. I didn't have time to consider what she meant.

Jarvis had settled sullenly in the corner, and Vasquez stalked through the room, barking the occasional order to the poor saps on the other end of his cell phone.

I opened my mouth to say something accusatory, then snapped it shut. Mason had been gone too long. His team hadn't reported back. Would we find them in time if I outed Jarvis? It was a risk.

A risk I couldn't take.

And before I could think through the situation enough to make sure that doing nothing for now was the best approach, an officer ran in and said something low to Vasquez. Vasquez barked a quick order and the cops started filing out of the building.

"Holmes, get back to the station," Vasquez ordered.

"What's going on?" I asked him.

He paused giving orders long enough to turn to me, and the worry behind the hardness guarding his expression hit me like a shot in the chest. "One of Mason's team radioed in. They've met some resistance. We've got officers en route. I need you to get back to the station."

The news was like a brick smashing into my stomach and I fought against the nausea that rolled through me. Resistance? Was Mason okay? I barely stopped myself from blurting out questions that Vasquez would have no answers for. I had to stay calm. I couldn't help him if I didn't stay calm.

I nodded to Vasquez when he glanced at me, but I kept my eyes on Jarvis. The imp walked quickly after the other officers. Staying just far enough away that he wouldn't notice my gaze, I followed him and the other officers out of the house.

Mason would be fine. He had to be. And if I rushed over there to help him, he wouldn't thank me. Not to mention the fact that I'd be too late to do much but hover over him. But I could still make a difference. Still help.

Mason's driveway and street parking had been almost entirely commandeered by the police. Jarvis was easy to keep in my sight as he ducked into his Ford Ranger. Most city-dwellers didn't drive pickups; he wouldn't be difficult to follow.

As the rest of the cops headed south—no doubt on their way to Mason's last known location—Jarvis went north. Exultation rushed through me and I turned to follow him. He drove unhurriedly toward his destination. Overly confident bastard.

I followed for a few miles until he turned off into an older part of town. A couple of miles and a few turns later and we were officially in one of the least pleasant Chicago suburbs. Old strip malls intermingled with unkempt houses and old apartment buildings, with a sprinkling of industrial structures for good measure.

Jarvis pulled into an abandoned strip mall parking lot, and I drove on, pulling into a convenience store next door. The truck disappeared and I parked and waited. Counting down five minutes by the clock on my dash, I struggled not to chew my nails in anticipation. When he didn't resurface, I got out of my car and walked around until I could observe the back of the strip mall. Jarvis was nowhere to be seen, but his truck was parked neatly at the back door of an old supermarket.

I closed my eyes and concentrated. The distance was at the limit of my range, but I was certain that I could sense anything with a significant power signature. The lycan energy jumped out at me first.

Mason.

Shit. What had they done? Taken him from the house they'd raided looking for Min? But why?

At this distance, I shouldn't have been able to say that it was him for sure. But we'd spent enough time together—grown close enough—that I was certain he was the lycan I sensed.

A darker power signature licked the edges of his, farther away from where I stood and watched. That one I couldn't confirm with any certainty, but I was willing to bet that it was Min's. Nearly overrun by the powerful vamp and lycan auras around him, Jarvis's imp aura drowned, a flicker of weak energy.

Two oh-dubs. I could easily handle a couple of humans with a gun, and probably an imp too. But the vamp would be a challenge. No. Going in alone would be stupid. Suicidal. But if the place was swarmed with cops and their sirens and flashing lights, then they might just kill Mason and go. Chances were, Jarvis carried a portable radio with him as well. So radio silence was imperative.

I pulled my cell phone out and hit Vasquez's name. Four rings and then he picked up.

"This isn't a good time, Holmes."

As quickly as I could, I told him the address and very specific instructions about radio silence. He was surprisingly silent on the other end of the line.

"You're sure he's in there?"

"Yes," I said simply.

"You maintain your distance until we get there. Twenty minutes, maybe thirty. I'll get some uniforms out there sooner."

"Okay."

"I'm serious, Astrid."

"I got it."

He cursed and the phone went dead. Despite what Vasquez feared, I knew I was outmatched. I'd wait it out. But Mason's face flashed in my mind. I had to get closer.

I pulled my 9mm out of the glove box where I'd stuffed it the first night I'd lost my badge and police-issued sidearm. I jogged to the back door of the grocery store and listened. Then I closed my eyes to allow my other senses to take the forefront of my mind. Mason's energy still rolled, but so did the others.

A cry, muffled by the door, snapped my eyes open. What were they doing in there? Were they hurting him? Killing him? I closed my eyes again, and his energy swirled and spiked unnaturally. I'd seen energy do that before. Not long before it faded into nothingness. If I waited for Vasquez to organize a rescue, would I lose Mason forever?

No.

I'd just found him. Against procedure or not, I had to get in there. Distract them. Something. Entering that building would mean putting my life on the line. It would mean that I cared enough about Mason to risk my life to spare his. Logically, I knew that he wouldn't thank me for it. But there was nothing else I could do. If I lost him when I could have saved him by distracting his torturers, I couldn't live with myself.

With trembling fingers, I touched my phone's screen. It would take Vasquez at least thirty minutes to get here. He'd said twenty, but there was no way. Not in traffic. Not even with lights flashing and sirens blaring. It was a long shot, but there was a small possibility that someone could get here sooner. If he was back in town.

I just had one more phone call to make. But the door was so close, I couldn't take the time to run back to the car to make sure the vampire inside didn't overhear me.

So, as quickly as I could, I sent a text message that I hoped my partner wouldn't be too far away to answer.

Chapter Thirteen

The handle of back door to the grocery store was locked, but not the deadbolt. A few quick motions with a credit card and I was in, gun in hand. The room I entered was dark, with small bits of light creeping in through mostly boarded-over windows. A dank smell touched my nose, mildew and bacteria-ridden stagnant water. I shut the door quietly behind me. Perspiration beaded on my forehead and between my breasts. Even though I couldn't detect much noise from my break-in, Min's ears would be far more sensitive.

But no vampire greeted me as I crept forward in the general direction of what I was certain was Mason's energy. I wished I could close my eyes to get a better fix, but that wasn't an option.

The back room I was in connected to the main store area through a short hallway with doors on either side. Old restrooms, by the signs on the doors. The air was oppressive, and the suffocating quality grew as I moved farther from the door. Dirt coated the floors. Some areas only a heavy sheen of dust, while others were marked where furnishings had been removed but the area beneath them hadn't been cleaned.

Other things were splattered on the floor as well. Dark stains coated in enough dust that it was difficult to tell their original color. Pink droplets I could almost convince myself had come from an old meat department in the grocery store, if they hadn't looked so fresh. Not days old, no. But maybe weeks. I wasn't much of a germaphobe, but I was almost willing to convert at the sight and smell of the old supermarket.

I crept into the hallway toward the main part of the store. A red stain, dark and almost hidden in the shadows, slid across small sections of the floor. My breath caught in my throat. Blood. Blood and what looked like drag marks.

My gun felt solid in my hands. Real. I thumbed off the safety and took another step. The shelving was still intact. I paused. Was that normal? It didn't seem like it. I'd thought they scavenged all they could when one of these places closed. Maybe the owner had thought including it would sell the property faster. Regardless of the reason, it made seeing anything all the more difficult.

Inky darkness bathed the room. Farthest from the front windows, and blocked from the back ones save for the hallway, the area was shadowed, and my mind jumped to fill the spaces with lunging imps and salivating vampires.

I risked a moment of lost focus to try to feel out which direction Mason was. Left, and still in front of me. Keeping my eyes darting and my gun fixed, I headed toward his familiar energy.

The smell hanging in the air went from dank to spoiled in the meat section. I didn't dare peek into the once-refrigerated bins, but I was certain that they hadn't been well cleaned after the supermarket closed. My feet were nearly silent against the dirty floor, but the slight tap of my shoe was audible—just barely—to my ears. The vampire—wherever she was—would certainly hear me coming.

My heart thudded against my chest at the thought, and my body tensed to run. To leave until backup could arrive. But I couldn't leave Mason here in this horrible, rank place alone. I couldn't leave him to die on the teeth of a vampire. I couldn't open a box tomorrow and find his accusing eyes staring back at me.

I forced myself forward and—gun first—rounded a corner into what must have been the fresh produce section. A fairly large amount of open space had large expanses of bins around it that once held potatoes and apples and onions. I'd made my way from the back to the front of the store. The light snaked in from the boarded up windows. And in the open space was a single, sturdy-looking chair, where a man was tied by his wrists and ankles to the heavy metal frame.

Mason looked up, moving his head slowly. Blood ran down his face and coated his neck and chest. Skin swollen and bruised, he was barely recognizable. And I could see punctures in his neck.

Our eyes met and recognition flashed in his eyes.

Suddenly one of the shadows moved, so quickly that I only registered the movement when the flash reached me. My gun flew from my hand and pain ripped up my arm and through my shoulder. I was face down on the ground, gun arm twisted behind my back before I could even squeak in protest.

The vampire yanked my other arm back and then pulled

me to my feet. A loud chuckle rolled through the air from behind me, masculine and arrogant. And Jarvis walked around to stand between me and Mason.

"Thank you for being so naïve and following me here, Astrid," he said. "And thanks for coming in when we called."

Min shoved me forward and I barely caught my footing before running headlong into Jarvis. I backed up a step when it looked like he was going to try to help me balance myself. Great. I'd not only walked right into a trap by following him, but I'd tightened the noose around my neck by coming in at the first hint that Mason was hurt. But I'd known that walking in. I hadn't come in here to take out a vampire and an imp. I'd walked into the building to distract them long enough for Mason to escape, and I hoped long enough for help to arrive.

"We need to finish this. She may have called in for back-up," Min said, voice humorless. What did Jarvis see in her? Oh right, a fellow homicidal maniac.

"You were a good cop, Jarvis," I said. I knew no such thing—he'd only been in our unit for a few months. But I figured he'd be easier to get talking. Help was on the way. I just had to keep us alive for a few more minutes. "Why are you doing this?"

"None of your business," Min said, simply. Jarvis gave her an annoyed glance, but didn't argue with her.

"I'm guessing money," I said, "because it can't be her sparkling personality."

Min simply gave me a smug grin, her menacing aura and vampiric energy swirling around her, coin flipping easily through her fingers. For a split second I lost myself in that energy, the swirl of shadows surrounding her, moving in their flowing, liquid way, before jerking back to reality.

"Then again, maybe you're the one who's slumming," I told her. "Come on, an imp?" I shrugged, doing my best to appear nonchalant. It might not fool a vampire, but Jarvis wouldn't be able to hear my thundering pulse.

"Bitch," Jarvis snapped, and pain exploded from my cheek.

I spit out a mouthful of blood and teetered on the edge of falling down. I'd gotten a reaction, if a bit more violent than what I had been looking for.

Keep them distracted.

"Well," I said thickly, "I get why she's doing it. Probably in love—or lust—with Nicolas." I shrugged, and pain ran up from the shoulder Min had wrenched. "But who could blame her. I mean, who could resist a powerful guy like that, when she goes home to an imp?"

I was ready for the strike this time, but it still hurt like hell. I fell to the ground, wrists screaming as I broke my fall with my hands. Blood dripped from my face to puddle on the ground. I tasted it on my tongue. And the flavor was almost a welcome change from the burnt coffee filling my nose. An angry, low growl filled the room, and I braced for another hit, but it didn't come.

"This is why I don't do field work," I said, my voice strangely thick. I blinked back the waves of darkness threatening to overcome me and looked up at my captors. But they were no longer watching me. Something moved behind them. Something shuddered and shook and groaned. Something was creating enough of a spike in Mason's aura to make concentrating fully on the scene nearly impossible, even with waves of pain rolling over me from every part of my body.

Lycan energy flooded the room, blinding me even as I tried to see what was happening. I pushed up from the ground and struggled to my knees, narrowing my eyes against the silver flood of power that only I could see even though I knew I wasn't seeing it with my physical eyes. And then I couldn't smell anything but fresh air and wide open spaces. And the energy shone even more. So radiant and sharp I almost lost my focus on him. On what was happening to him.

Mason's scream shook me to my core. Agony and fury and triumph. All rolled into one terrible sound. His arms flexed against his bindings, and waves moved beneath his skin like water in the ocean. Land rolling in an earthquake.

Like an animal, his fingers stretched and clawed at the chair, but he didn't seem to be trying to get free that way. It was more like the pain of whatever was happening to him was too much to bear without movement.

What was wrong with him? My mind flashed to a spell that could be hurting him so much, but I dropped the idea as soon as it surfaced. I knew what was happening, I just couldn't believe it.

He was shifting.

The years Mason had avoided his change—bottled it— should have prevented this. Should have made it impossible. A lycan who hadn't changed in years could no longer change alone. Could no longer change without the full moon above and a pack to help. Could definitely not change under a half moon—during the day, no less—while hurt and nearly unconscious.

But there was no denying what was happening in front of my eyes.

Mason's skin stretched and his bones popped and

cracked, moving into new positions. Skin broke, and I cried out when blood poured from the wounds that appeared. Wounds that only healed when fur pushed out from beneath his skin.

The vampire was shouting something at the imp, but Jarvis seemed hypnotized by the sight. Min started toward Mason, and I realized that I had to do something. Anything. If she reached him mid-change, he would have no chance. He'd be unable to defend himself.

I searched the floor desperately for my gun. Finally, I spotted it. Mason growled, loud and long. Min stood over him. Jarvis still appeared stunned and oblivious to anything but Mason. Over the filthy floor, I lunged for the gun. My fingers closed over the cold, reassuring steel.

I didn't hesitate.

My aim from the floor wasn't great, and I had normal rounds loaded in my gun, but I got two good hits to the vampire's shoulder. One second, blood splashed from her shoulder, and the next, Min was standing over me. Rage coated her face and her pretty features were transformed into something truly ghastly.

I tried to swing my gun up, but ran into solid vampire. Solid, pissed vampire. I didn't see her move again, but the agony shooting from my neck was very real. Someone cried out in pain.

It might have been me.

It felt like Min was chewing through to my bone. Then the vampire was gone, though the sting radiating from my neck didn't fade. Min flew across the room, and I heard metal breaking and plastic and glass shattering.

And I looked into the eyes of the beast.

Mason as a man was hard and handsome, but the word beautiful would never have occurred to me to describe him. But as a fully changed lycanthrope, there was no other word that fit. But it was a terrible beauty. Tawny hair covered his body, and his eyes—still the dark gray I'd come to rely on so much in the last few days—flashed with animalistic fury. Muscles flexed and moved under his fur—muscles that were different from those of any animal or man.

His arms were far too long for his still-bipedal body, and the claws at the end of them looked as sharp as razor blades. I should have been afraid. Lycans who turned after so long as humans had a harder time with control and were more prone to blackouts and rages. But I saw *him* in those eyes. And I could never be afraid of Mason.

Mason jerked, and I pushed myself up from the ground. Jarvis was on Mason's back, holding on by a knife he'd plunged between the lycan's shoulder blades. Imps weren't particularly strong, but they were fast as hell, and sneaky. Jarvis flung himself from Mason and skittered away into the darkness.

"We have to get out of here." I choked out the words, hoping Mason could understand between my swollen mouth and his lycan form. Mason turned to look at me, his eyes widened and then narrowed into an even more intense rage. I must look like hell.

A growl escaped him and he jumped to the side, revealing Jarvis at his back again. Knife in hand, an evil glee danced through the imp's eyes. Being with Min hadn't changed Jarvis into a psychopath. I bet he'd been that way for a very long time.

Suddenly Min was there too, lips drawn back to reveal bloody fangs and swinging a large piece of metal—an old shelf by the looks of it—at Mason. They ignored me. Rightly assuming that I wasn't the real threat in the room.

I swung my gun up but I couldn't get a safe shot in. Finally Mason spun around quickly and Jarvis pulled back, knife back in the imp's hand from between Mason's ribs. Jarvis was quick as hell, but he'd tuned me out and was looking for another opening to stab Mason again. Blood ran down the knife and Jarvis bared his teeth. Mason cried out in pain.

I fired.

The imp went down like a stone. Clean chest shot.

Mason and Min fought, still so fast it was difficult to see who was winning. But they were both tiring. Both wounded and bleeding all over the stained floor. Their energy swirled and mixed with the imp's fading aura, adding to my confusion.

Mason backhanded the vampire and a *crack* sounded, harsh and loud. Min faltered and fell back, dazed.

"Stay there, Min," I shouted, finding my voice somewhere in the surreal fog rolling through my mind. I aimed right at her fangs.

She wouldn't survive a headshot in her condition. She had to know that. Barely able to maintain her footing, she raised her arms slightly—a short, quick movement of defeat.

And then her head was gone.

I didn't see the vampire coming from behind her. Nor did I see the quick motion he used to tear Min's head from her body. All I saw was the aftermath. Blood spurting from Min's neck as her heart continued to pump, unaware that it was dead. Her body, falling in slow motion.

And Luc Chevalier. Holding Min's head in his hands.

Chapter Fourteen

The police showed up less than a minute after Luc decapitated Min, and the sudden influx of people and sirens and
questions and noise pushed me into a state of pure shock.
I couldn't keep focused, and I found myself next to Mason,
holding him as his transformation reversed. The reversal
was just as horrifying and painful as the initial change, and I
feared for his life.

Despite the blood and terror and hustle of people
around me, I clung to him. Then the rush of energy from the
oh-dubs around us was overwhelming. The people faded,
and only the energy remained.

Vasquez's voice roused me Not because he was yelling—
that might have been normal enough to ignore. But because
he was talking softly. Reassuring me. Asking me to let Mason
go.

My hands clung to him. Pressing against the wounds I
could get to in an inane attempt to stop the flow of blood.

I found it strange that the wounds caused by the change from man into lycan and vice versa healed as soon as the transformation was complete, but other wounds remained. Frustrated scientists probably struggled with the same issue. Vasquez gently pulled me away, and carried me to a gurney. The insanity of that moment penetrated my shock, and suddenly I couldn't get the words out fast enough.

"How is he? Where are they taking him? God, he took off her head." I babbled, and Vasquez reassured me that everything would be okay, as EMTs carted me to the ambulance. Despite my protests, a paramedic gave me something to relax. And the world faded away.

I awoke in the hospital. And although I was certain that no more than a few hours had passed, Claude sat at my bedside.

"How is he?" I croaked out.

My partner reached out, water-filled cup in hand, and had me take a drink from the straw. I took a quick sip and the cool water was like a lozenge on my throat. "Claude," I insisted, my voice stronger for the moisture.

"He's fine. Or he will be. He's in surgery now, but you can see him after. Your injuries are treated. They may even let you go home today. But you'll be feeling those cracked ribs and that broken nose for a while."

As if summoned by Claude's words, pain suddenly flared from my wounds. My whole body ached—my ribs especially when I took a breath. My face hurt. And I was forced to breathe through my mouth. A bandage covered my nose.

"I'll get a nurse to give you another shot—"

"Wait," I said. Realizing how nasally I sounded, I lowered my voice. "Tell me what happened. After. And how did you get here so damn fast?"

"I flew out immediately after you texted and then wouldn't answer your phone."

I grimaced, and pain spiked through my face.

"You scared the hell out of me, Astrid. I got your text with the address and your ominous message that you were going in, and that I needed to take care of Charlie if you didn't come out. Then when you wouldn't answer your phone…" He shook his head.

"You called Luc." It wasn't a question, not really. I'd texted Claude out of desperation, knowing that he probably wouldn't be back in town yet. But I'd relied on him for so long, I knew that if I could count on anyone to help me rescue Mason, it would be him.

"Of course I did."

"You were certain you could trust him?"

"To help you, if he could get there in time? Yes. But his methods aren't what I would have hoped for."

Luc had killed Min. I'd killed Jarvis. No witnesses. Nothing concrete to tie Nicolas to any crime. Was that why the Magister had killed Min?

The question must have flashed across my face. "I don't know why Luc killed her. But he's claiming that he was worried for your lives. It's not something I think we can disprove. And…"

"And?"

"Luc and Nicolas are claiming that Min killed Jake of her own volition, because she wanted to see Nicolas happy. Then she killed Mary because she decided she wasn't good enough for Nicolas." He shook his head. "Hell, Luc has gone so far as to suggest that he invited Isaiah to come take care of Min. That she'd gotten out of control. Although he, of course, didn't realize how far gone she really was."

I laughed, a short humorless sound that I regretted as pain spiked from my ribs. "That makes no sense. They're just making that up to remove Nicolas from suspicion. How are they explaining Jarvis's involvement? And if that's true about Isaiah, why didn't he tell us that when we spoke to him?"

"They're saying Jarvis was in it for the money. And he was sleeping with Min. Both of those give him good reason to help her. As far as Isaiah is concerned, since Luc wasn't willing to come out and say anything about him directly, I don't think we'll get a straight answer there. And we don't have anything to charge Isaiah with either. The evidence just isn't there to charge him with the other victims the OWEA is certain are his. So he's hardly inspired to talk to us about anything."

"But it's all bullshit, Claude." For once, my mom's voice didn't reverberate through my mind at the curse. "What happened to Min's coin?"

He grimaced. "Some witches came and looked at it. It's in evidence right now, but the Covenant is petitioning for it. Something about ancient, dangerous magic that needs to be destroyed. They claim that the enchantment on the coin is old. It's probably been enchanted for the centuries that Min has carried it, and might have been that way since before she owned it."

Destroyed? Far more likely the coin would find its way into a witch's research. A permanently enchanted object was a thing of legends. A lot of witches would be interested in seeing how it was accomplished. "What does Vasquez say about all this?"

"He's buying most of it. My guess is that he just wants this mess of a case closed. He knows we don't have enough to charge Nicolas. He's not willing to make a stink about it when he knows we can't prove any of it in court." He grinned. "He's pretty pissed at you, though. Something about not obeying a direct order. I don't think he'll fire you, your powers are too valuable. But I'd imagine you'll get very familiar with your desk for a good long while."

Relief rushed through me at that. I might not love the field, but I did love my job. After seeing Mason tied to that chair, and facing down Min and Jarvis, nothing sounded so good as my nice, safe desk. At least for a while. And Min and Jarvis were gone. They'd never hurt anyone again.

But it wasn't good enough.

"He did this, Claude. Nicolas was behind all of this. I know it."

"I know. And Nicolas won't get away with this, Astrid." His eyes narrowed. "But you'll just have to trust me on that."

Annoyance ran through me. But we'd gotten Jake and Mary Stone's killers. Even if the one directing them was beyond my ability to take down for the moment. "But Mason's all right," I said, reassuring myself more than asking him.

Claude grinned, and the room brightened. "Yes, little one. Your werewolf is going to be okay."

The nurses let me in to talk to the very drugged, very irritated Mason. I stayed by his bedside until I feared that if I didn't get a shower, I'd soon be booted out of the hospital.

And I worried that even though he wasn't really talking to me, that my presence was keeping him from resting fully. He muttered and groaned in his sleep. I went home and showered, then collapsed into bed. Claude had promised to stop by Mason's and feed Charlie. I didn't ask how he would get in. And aside from me, Claude was Charlie's favorite person. I rested easier knowing that someone would be looking after the cat. The next morning, I woke before dawn.

I blinked at the grayness of predawn shining into my bedroom and tried to pinpoint what woke me. I closed my eyes and felt with my mind. Flashing with wildness and so familiar I had to blink back tears, lycan energy pulled at me. And the fresh scent of outdoors and sunshine filled my nose.

Then the doorbell rang.

I trotted down the stairs as quickly as I could on my still-sore ankle and with every movement sending pulses of pain from my face, and sharp spikes from my cracked ribs. I opened the door without a glance out the peephole, and threw my arms around Mason's chest, taking care to keep my bandaged nose a few inches away from his broad chest.

He jerked in my arms and I jumped back. "I'm so sorry. Are you okay? What are you doing here?"

His face was ashen and dark circles rimmed his eyes, but the strength he always carried with him remained. Beaten down, but never beaten.

"He threatened to walk here." Claude's voice was tight with disapproval, and he stood behind Mason. A frown creased his ever-young face. "I'll be back in an hour." Then with the speed Claude rarely demonstrated in front of non-vampires, he was gone.

I helped Mason into the house. He supported himself

okay, but I worried, so I clung to his arm and led him to the couch. I sat beside him, and he melted into the squishy furniture.

"You look terrible." And he did. Bruises and cuts covered far too much of his swollen face. And the T-shirt he'd forced on did little to cover his bandages.

"Right back at you." He grinned to soften the insult.

I touched my nose softly. "What on Earth are you doing here?" I demanded. "I was heading back to the hospital in an hour." Sudden guilt rose in my chest to clog my throat. "I'm sorry. I should have been there when you woke up."

He shook his head slowly. "Nonsense. I'm the one who should apologize. But I just had to see…had to make sure."

I took his hand in mine and gave him a reassuring squeeze. I understood just how he felt. I'd needed to see him too. Had to make certain—with my own eyes—that he was okay.

"You changed," I said, and his gaze snapped back to mine.

"Yes."

"How did you do that?"

"I'm not entirely sure. It shouldn't even be possible. But when I saw him hit you, it was like the beast poured out of me. The thought of you getting hurt—killed—was more than I could handle. When he hit you, a fever overtook me and the power I haven't felt in years rolled over me. Forced its way out of me."

He took a haggard breath. "When we went in after Min, she was waiting for us. She dropped some sort of blinding grenade on us—a spell bought from a witch, I think. Caused enough confusion that she got the drop on us. I watched her take down the rest of my team, Astrid, before they knocked me out and dragged me to that old building. A couple might make it, but I didn't know that at the time. I knew that she'd kill you without a second thought. I couldn't let you die."

"They kept you alive to draw me out."

"Yes. Min still thought you might be able to identify her off the coin. Or even off of Mary Stone. She didn't want to take chances."

I reached out and smoothed his bed-smooshed hair. He let me, eyes still searching my face and his hands squeezing my other hand.

"Astrid, if I'd lost you—"

"Hush," I said gently. "You didn't."

"Please. I have to say this. If I'd lost you, I don't know how I would have gone on. I should have told you this a year ago. I should have pushed past my own issues to talk to you. I should have asked you out on a damn date."

I smiled at him but no amusement broke his pained expression.

"I care about you, Astrid. Your kindness and your warmth. Your clever brain and your courage." He took a haggard breath. "And I love the way you look at me. With so much trust and affection."

It was too soon to say more. I knew that, even if the words screamed inside my chest. And even though I knew Mason was different, a small part of me—buried deep inside—still feared that he'd end up like my parents; that someday he'd decide that I wasn't worth caring about.

But the rest of me knew better. And the rest of me didn't care how much it would hurt if he left, because that part of me knew he never would.

"I care about you, too." I steeled my spine. "But if you want to be with me, you're going to have to put the guilt over what happened to your fiancé behind you." He winced but I pressed on. Not only talking to him anymore. Natalie's words pressed against my mind. I needed to reach out to my family, too. See if there was a connection that could be bridged. "You almost died yesterday. Something could happen to you—could happen to any of us—at any time." My throat tried to close at the thought. "Do you really want to risk never seeing your family again? Do they deserve that?"

He shook his head, and my heart sank. But he wasn't denying the truth of my words. "You're right," he said, voice thick.

"Of course I am." I smiled at him brightly, and he grinned back. I leaned forward and kissed him softly. A few days for Mason to recover, and maybe, just maybe, I'd finally get a chance to start the life I'd always wanted. One with a person who really cared about me. Broken bones aside, it was going to be a darn good week.

Acknowledgments

There are so many people I owe a thank you for their help and encouragement with this project, and who have been supportive of my writing in general. I want to give a huge thanks to:

First my readers, thank you for everything!

My family, for always being there for me, and for supporting my choice to try this writing thing. I love you all so much! Especially my husband, Sash, who accepts my crazy writing hours in stride, and has been willing to entertain himself virtually every evening and weekend for the last two years. And my mom, who always remains stalwart in her belief that I can do anything I set my mind to. Thank you for believing in me.

My editor, Kerry Vail, for being a marvelous editor and friend. You have been my biggest cheerleader and my rock, and you have helped me grow so much as a writer. More than that, you've been such a good friend. There are no words to express how much your support means to me.

My critique partner, Regan Summers, who not only inspires me with her insight and her amazing writing, but whose friendship keeps me sane. You encourage me when I need to be encouraged, and kick me in the butt when I need that, too. And Joshua Roots, who offers sage advice when it comes to improving my stories, and who encourages me with his own tenacity and hilarious writing. Thank you, my friends. And thanks to the rest of the Cantina crew, for always giving me a fun place full of support.

Barbara Rogan, for your encouraging words and invaluable teachings. And the rest of my Next Level workshop group, for helping me strengthen my writing and for your kind and supportive words. You are all talented and awesome.

Editors Erin McCormack Molta, Heather Howland, Stacy Abrams, and Kerri-Leigh Grady for your help in making this series the best it could be.

The rest of the Entangled team, for seeing potential in my stories and helping me develop and market them. Special thanks to Misa Ramirez for her constant kindness and hard work, and to my publicists Jessica Turner and Katie Clapsadl. Thanks so much for everything!

About the Author

CPA-turned-romance-author Tiffany Allee used to battle spreadsheets in Corporate America, and now concentrates on her characters' battles to find love. Raised in small-town Colorado, Tiffany currently lives in Phoenix, AZ, by way of Chicago and Denver. She is happily married to a secret romantic who tolerates her crazy mutterings.

She writes about ass-kicking heroines and the strong heroes who love them. Her work includes the suspense-driven *Otherworlder Enforcement Agency* series which revolves around a group of paranormal cops solving crimes and finding love, and *Don't Bite the Bridesmaid*, a lighthearted paranormal romance (Entangled Publishing).

Tiffany has an MBA in accounting and nearly a decade of experience in corporate finance. All super useful stuff for a writer who spends far too much time trying to figure out fun ways to keep her characters apart, and interesting ways to kill people (for her books—of course!). http://tiffanyallee.com